Gulf Dreams

DATE DUE

Gulf Dreams

Emma Pérez

Third Woman Press
Berkeley

This book would not have been possible without the support of the Ethnic Studies Department of the University of California, Berkeley.

Typeset by Get Set! Prepress, Oakland, Calif.
Printed and bound by McNaughton & Gunn, Lithographers, Saline, Mich.

Cover art: *La Mestiza*, monotype, by Beatriz Pestana.

Acknowledgements
Penguin Books, New York: from *Story of the Eye*, by Georges Bataille, 1982.
Carcanet, Manchester, England: from *The Hour of the Star*, by Clarice Lispector, 1986.
Fondo de Cultura Economica, México, D.F.: from *Migraciones*, by Gloria Gervitz, 1991.

First printing October 1996
96 97 98 99 10 9 8 7 6 5 4 3 2 1

Library of Congress Cataloging-in-Publication Data

Pérez, Emma, 1954-
  Gulf dreams / Emma Pérez.
        p.   cm.
    ISBN 0-943219-13-2
    I. Title.
  PS3566.E691324G85   1996   95-48814
    813' .54—dc20   CIP

Many friends read unfinished drafts as I experimented with this manuscript. Thank you for your insights, confidence, and love: Gloria Anzaldúa, Bonnie Brown, Yolanda Broyles-González, Antonia Castañeda, Georgia Cottrell, Teresa de Lauretis, Deena González, Nicolás Kanellos, Chéla Sandoval, Rosario Sanmiguel, Carla Trujillo, and Yvonne Yarbro-Bejarano. At Third Woman Press, Norma Alarcón saw promise in the first pages years before I could envision an ending; Ellie Hernández has been vigilant and patient; Kathrine Ramirez offered her reflections. At UTEP, my history department has been encouraging. In Austin, Cynthia Pérez y Las Manitas fed me tacos and friendship. Antes de todos, mi mamá y mi papá, Emma y José Pérez, siempre me han regalado su inspiración.

para Yolanda, Cristelia, Sonja y José Roberto
mis hermanas y mi hermano

para Rosario, por su fé

y para Ché, por supuesto

Confession

Thus it was that our sexual dream
kept changing into a nightmare.

Story of the Eye
Georges Bataille

I met her in my summer of restless dreams. It was a time when infatuation emerges erotic and pure in a young girl's dreams. She was a small girl, a young woman. Her eyes revealed secrets, mysteries I yearned to know long after that summer ended.

My eldest sister introduced us. The young woman, the sister of my sister's best friend, became my friend. At our first meeting we went to the park. We walked, then stood under a tree for hours exchanging glances that bordered on awkward embarrassment. I remember we avoided the clarity of the afternoon. In a few moments, after her eyes sunk tenderly into mine, she caressed a part of me I never knew existed.

At fifteen, I hadn't known love. I don't know if I fell in love that day. I know I felt her deeply and reassuringly. Without a touch, her passion traced the outline of my face. I wanted to brush her cheek lightly with my hand, but I, too frightened, spoke in riddles, euphemistic yearnings: the sun so hot, the trees so full, the earth pressed beneath me.

Weeks passed before I saw her again. During those nights, I dreamt but did not sleep. Lying in my bed next to an open window, the breezes aroused me. They made me feel a peculiar edginess mixed with calm. It rained. A soft drizzle fell on my face through the netted screen. I dreamt of her fingers brushing my skin, lightly smoothing over breasts, neck, back, all that ached for her. A fifteen-year-old body ached from loneliness and desire, so unsure of the certainties her body felt. Nights like this would bring her to me. Never sleeping. Half-awake to ensure that it was she embracing me. In those dreams we touched carefully. By morning, I rose exhausted. For those few weeks, sleepless, restless dreams exhausted me.

The day I would see her again held me in fear and anticipation. Far more than these emotions, I felt relief. To see her would satisfy me, if only momentarily. Again, my body spoke to me. To see her eyes envelope mine. I had to remember their color. I had to see the olive hands that caused so much delight. I had to know that I had not invented her for dreams.

It was morning. A hot, dusty, gravel road linked our homes. My eldest sister drove to the young girl's house to call on her own best friend. I sat, the passenger, staring out at fields, rows of cotton balls, white on green, passing quickly, the motion dizzying my head and stomach. My sister, familiar with my nausea in moving vehicles, had wrapped a wet face cloth in a plastic bag. The coolness of the moist rag soothed my forehead. As an additional precaution I had stuffed two brown paper bags, one inside the other, under the car seat.

When we arrived, she was swinging on a porch swing hanging from a worn, wooden house, the paint peeling with no memory of color. Our sisters hugged, went into the kitchen, poured coffee and prepared for gratifying gossip. We were not alone: brothers, sisters, a mother, faces and names I can't recall — the introductions necessary, trusting, unsuspecting. No one knew why I had come. To see my new friend, they thought. To link families with four sisters who would be friends longer than their lifetimes through children who would bond them at baptismal rites. Comadres. We would become intimate friends sharing coffee, gossip and heartaches. We would endure the female life-cycle — adolescence, marriage, menopause, death, and even divorce, before or after menopause, before or after death.

I had not come for that. I had come for her kiss.

We walked through tall grass. Silent. A path led to the shade of a tree. Her waist and hips, rhythmic, broad, swaying. At sixteen, her hips and breasts were that of a woman. Under the tree, we avoided eyes, avoided touch, avoided that which I hoped we both wanted. I stared at her, mirroring her black eyes. We sat on moist earth. She grabbed handfuls of dry leaves, sifting them through her fingers, methodically repeating her exercise. For an instant, I forgot her name. I couldn't place her. She was foreign, a stranger. The memory loss buffered my pain. So painful to admit the distance between us. I left that day without renewal. I knew the dreams would cease. I began to repair the damage. I revived the mundane. I sought its refuge.

The dreams did not cease. I saw her with him. That day under the shaded tree, she had spoken about a young boy. She craved his delicious, expert mouth, she said. She told me he had sucked her nipples. He was careful not to hurt her or impregnate her. Instead, he licked her moistness. He loved her. No other boy had ever licked her softness.

Those were my dreams. The morning I lost my memory, forgot her name, I revered the lips that relived desire for him. At night, they appeared in my bedroom. Invaded my bed. Even there, she belonged to him.

I didn't envy him. I despised him, his coarseness, his coarse, anxious determination. She longed for someone to arouse her. Each time she dared to look directly into my eyes, she quickly averted hers. She alerted the passion, repressed it immediately. Her fear, a reproach against me. Still, I wanted her. I wanted her to come alone at night just as she had those first two weeks when exhaustion fulfilled me.

We became friends. The promise of female rituals enraged me. We met weekly, then monthly, then not at all. Her boy became her cause. Often, I spotted him in the fields. His strong, brown back bending over to pick the cotton that filled the trailing sack. A perfectly beautiful back, I thought. She was in love with a beautifully strong, muscular, brown back.

As a young woman of fifteen in a rural Texas coastal town, I didn't recognize love. In a town where humidity bred hostility, I memorized hate. Bronze in the summer with hair and eyes so light that I could pass through doors that shut out my sisters and brother. Their color and brown eyes, I envied. I grew to resent the colors that set me apart from my family. At four, my sisters convinced me I was adopted. Eyes so green, this was not my family. At five, I took a butcher knife, sat calmly, sadly, on the pink chenille bedspread, threatening to slice away at tanned skin. I remember the scene like a dream. Always the sad child, burdened.

When I stared into cameras, I didn't laugh or clown as children do, so unfamiliar to me how my cousins giggled with each other. My mother framed photographs that captured the sadness, held it squarely like a package with a time bomb that would not explode for years. Right now, the sadness glared. There was one photograph. Not yet one-year-old and I laughed openly and happily. Evidence of childhood. I wondered, when did the sadness begin?

Pronunciation divided worlds. In a school where students' names ranged from Hodges and Hutchins to a sprinkling of Garza and González, teachers rejected Spanish sounds. They taught me to enunciate strange foreign words, immigrant sounds.

With a sweet southern drawl, the teacher taught English to Mexican children.

"Church," she said.

"Shursh," I repeated.

"Church," she spoke, slower, louder.

"Shursh," I pronounced, quickly, softly.

Unskilled at the language of survival, but I would learn.

This happens when the senses are unaware. Language must be mouthed from a child's lips, to speak violence, but instead mimicry is learned and the child is silenced.

❏

I missed her. Daily, hourly, I missed her. Since that meeting under the tree, I had retrieved pride to dismiss longing. The pride surfaced. It guided me through the day. It stopped me from climbing into my sister's white Dodge. Weekly, my sister traveled that gravel road to confer with her comadre.

One Saturday morning, I tucked away pride, answered longing, and sat the passenger, the victim. She half-expected me. Took my hand, led me to her bedroom, shoved me playfully on her twin bed next to her. She spoke reasonably. She had missed me. Why had I stopped coming? Why had I stayed away? She relied on my friendship, a passionate friendship, she called it. Mute, I looked away, paralyzed, embarrassed, hurt. She played at my emotions under the guise of friendship. We had moved far beyond that first day when we refused to acknowledge clarity.

A knock on the door, the interruption inevitable. Through the door, her mother announced his intrusion. He waited on the porch swing, waited to take her for a ride in a borrowed black Chevy, waited to drive her to deserted fields and back roads where boys tested their virility.

Her eyes sparkled. He gave them an amused sparkle. She examined my face, searching for jealousy. Since an early age, I learned to exhibit indifference with sad eyes. She misinterpreted the sadness and chose jealousy. I peered from her window. The angle framed them, froze them like a photograph, his arm around her waist. The black Chevy rolled away, rocks crackling under the wheels, dust spreading, leaving a brown film on my sister's white Dodge.

I would not see her again for a year.

My mother's house rested behind my father's workshop. My older sisters told me there had been a house before this one where they and my brother had lived. I only lived there until my first birthday. Then, my father moved us closer to the railroad tracks, next to the cotton gin.

I memorized the routine of caring in that two-bedroom home for six people. My cousins supposed we were rich to live in a house my father bought with the G.I. bill. They lived in time-worn rented houses. Ours was newer but hidden behind an aluminum building, my father's upholstery shop, my favorite playground. Among the stripped chairs and couches waiting for floral designs to hide the bare frames, among the velour scraps and sharp nails, my brother and I played. My father's hammering was our financial security, his love proven over and over. Sometimes he hammered for sixteen hours daily, pausing only for ice water and Saltine crackers. My brother and I were messengers, carriers, delivering our mother's tenderness to our father down a worn path from the house to the shop.

I distrusted and even despised some brown-skinned men when I was fifteen. But I loved my father. A broad-shouldered man with black, curly hair, he adored my mother's beauty. He raged jealously when she paraded into town with her sisters. Men would admire her creamy light skin, curved waist and hips, her thick, black hair. She feared my father's jealousy like abuse, and often stayed home to appease. I misunderstood her compliance. In time, I recognized her strength, his weakness.

Before the summer of restless dreams, I watched my sisters dress, paint their cheeks and lips, file nails, and emerge perfumed and shapely for brown-skinned boys. They each picked one. The eldest chose a small, cynical one. The younger chose a dark, brooding boxer. They would both become my friends. They would both deceive my sisters and lose my trust. Men and deception became one fused realization. Yet, like myself, they only sought understanding — selfish, understanding and constant adoration from women.

My brother, the necessary companion throughout childhood. *Los cuates*, the twins, our family named us. Inseparable. He, small-boned, petite, eternally naive, was younger than I in every way but years. Accustomed to his companionship, I resented how he shunned my invitations to films or parties as we grew older. Maybe he resented me. I, bigger, lighter-skinned, had caught up with him in school, made friends and passing grades. Maybe I reminded him too much of the white world outside our home. Maybe in mastering the language of survival, I too became an outsider. He no longer allowed me to share his hopes. Long before, I had ceased listening.

At fifteen, I didn't hate boys. I even liked some of them. Between the young gigglers with hard-ons and the older cat-callers with hard-ons, the choices were few. Finally, I chose one. I chose an outsider, white-skinned, blue-eyed, so blond his hair was white. In two years together through daily phone calls, weekly films, and obligatory kisses, I refused to let him inside. Years later, after we ended daily phone calls, when his wife was at work, I mounted him as he lay on his living room floor. Too guilty to take me to a white woman's bed, too ashamed to make love, his face flushed. In seconds, it was over. A beginning and an end were wrapped in one humiliating afternoon. The afternoon on his living room floor punctuated the end of a romance. The end mimicked the beginning.

When I was fifteen and chose him, he released a numbness that had protected me from her. The protection gone, the numbness lifted, the dreams revived, she returned alone at night to soothe, to nurture, to explain why we loved only in dreams. I fell deeper. She would never leave, not as long as he stayed. Now she protected me from passage into female rites.

He wore pain. His face a grimace, his voice unctuous. He loved to wear pain. A young boy of seventeen from Alabama, he mistrusted his mother's anger. He and his father colluded. They misunderstood her thick, white body, her callused hands, her bitterness. Domestic service in Alabama was a black women's work. In Texas, Mexican women cleaned white women's homes. Her white skin had not guaranteed that privilege.

She did not marry above her family. She married a poor boy, a hard worker like herself. The man she married spotted a strong build for healthy babies and a double salary. He raised her son to despise her strength. The son took her bitterness and made it his own. How could she have measured her son's deception? He would bond with male prerogative to abandon the female, the womb.

When I met him, I inherited his contempt for a mother he neither respected nor pitied. I inherited him the moment when a boy's ambivalence turns cocksure. Arrogance takes over, tenderness cannot be public. Maleness, so convinced of its superiority to the feminine, evolves.

Instinctively, relationships became predictable, and I became cold, withdrawn. Only she could break through. I resisted as long as I could. Frozen. Her glance, a playful word would melt me. Once again, longing disrupted me.

The year without her, before age sixteen, I preoccupied myself with the boy from Alabama. The town disapproved of brown and white holding hands. Since my childhood, racial insults were common in supermarkets, restaurants, laundromats, barber shops, and gas station bathrooms. The Texaco near my grandmother's house announced on its bathroom door, "For Colored Only."

In the first grade, two six-year-olds worried that Russian airplanes might bomb the school. My enemy languished across the aisle whispering to an accomplice. Two blonde, big-boned girls conspired as they judged brown skin. Their parents had told them to keep away from Mexicans with *piojos*; lice that hatched from eggs exploded like little bombs in hair, bearers of filth and disgust. Unlike my friends Josefina y Susana, I wasn't defiant. Josie and Susie would run up close to the *bolillitas* and shove a brown head of hair next to a blonde one and then run away. The white girls would scream; my friends would rejoice, victorious at the game they invented to balance injustices. But the game only lasted on the playground. In class, the Anglo teacher handed crisp, new chalk sticks to the white students who wore freshly pressed cotton. They filed to the black board, proudly, scribbling answers to multiplication tables. The Mexicans remained seated in desks lining the back wall of the room, too shy to cross the aisles, approach the front and sharpen dull pencils.

Josie and Susie were my closest friends, but a girl who wandered home, alone, each day, lived in a brick home where the rich *bolillos* lived, became another kind of friend. She dressed in green, red and blue plaid dresses, not hand-me-downs. Her hair shone black accented by blue hues. When I overheard the *bolillas* talking about her, I realized this strange girl was an outcast, like me. I wondered why they couldn't accept her, until I heard them whisper, "She's a Jesus-killer."

Sue and I became friends who barely spoke. Our silent pledge defied children's cruel jokes. Josie and Susie didn't want me to walk or sit beside Sue, she's too weird, they'd say, she's not Mexican, doesn't speak Spanish, they criticized. But I recognized a loner, a quiet self-contained girl who didn't have friends and didn't seem to care. Our friendship was restricted to holding hands on the playground. Afternoons, I'd traverse the railroad tracks with Josie and Susie to the same poor neighborhood. They'd mimic kids on the sidewalk — the way they walked or talked. I joked with them. They didn't bother me about Sue anymore. It was as if they understood that she and I were alike in some off-colored way.

❑

I spotted her in a local market. The clerk, an elderly Anglo from Louisiana, harassed her. She placed a loaf of white bread on the counter. He refused to add the thirty-three cents to her family's account. Their payment was late again. She argued with him, then pleaded. Finally, the store manager, a middle-aged, pot-bellied man, the clerk's son, stepped up to the check-out stand. His eyes swallowed firm, young breasts. Her smile convinced him. Promptly, he added thirty-three cents to her bill. She had begun payment with a smile. It found her in his shabby, filthy, office on a cot that stunk like mildew. I judged her. I would continue to judge her until I stripped for men whose power robbed my integrity.

That night, I spy her on the store manager's cot, lying on her stomach, her buttocks smooth and firm. His hand moved across her back, finding a heart-shaped ass. He rubbed up and down, then in circles, enjoying her muscular flesh. But it was I who kissed her eyes and she who licked my nipples with her tongue. Awakened, I quivered. I felt her go to him, her boy, the one she nurtured. I felt her loving him again. She would not leave him easily. I knew that.

Routine and books comforted me. The summer over, fall gave me hope. I studied. I sublimated. I worked at K-Mart.

Patterns from the past still paint my future. I sought protection. I realize now his white skin stood like armor between me and an unjust town. I liked this boy from Alabama whose blue eyes witnessed poverty in his own home. I liked his big shoulders, his tight, freckled forearms. We became lovers who kissed on Friday nights at drive-in theaters, where I avoided sex.

His demands doubled. He gave orders. My resistance led to petty arguments, so typically the high school sweethearts' drama. He was muscular, popular, a straight-A white student;

I was Mexican, smart and somewhat pretty. After a year, his habits bored me. The kisses no longer stimulated. My eyes wandered to neighborhood boys, to *pachucos*, so coolly sexy, so dangerously off-limits. My eyes wandered but at night I waited for her.

I had always loved her. The moment I saw her again, my heart sank. I fought tears. She had grown more beautiful. Being in love, I thought, has made her more beautiful. Her hair fell around her face. We had not spoken since that day in her bedroom. Smiling, she drifted toward me. Trying to return the smile, my lips pursed stiffly. My expression puzzled her. When she hugged me, she buried her head between my neck and shoulder, resting comfortably, feeling familiar in each other's arms.

The smell of her hair, I had only imagined its scent. She asked how I had been. She had spied on me often, she said, at school, the park, in town, with the boy from Alabama. Questioning me, she sought answers. Was I happy? Did I love him? Her voice bubbled. Quickly, I masked emotions, hiding behind him, pretending he was special. I don't think I lied when I said I loved him. I hid behind that kind of love. But the sight of her reminded me I had only practiced at love. I practiced kisses and language with him. The smell of her hair woke me.

I'd never touched her. I carried her inside me, imagined entering her, enjoying that ration of her, when and if she wanted me.

I couldn't compete with her past, nor could she with mine. There was no competition, only commonality. Our souls touched before in a life where my love for her was not forbidden.

How can I explain she was the core of me? I repeat this over and over, to you, to myself. We merged before birth, entwined in each other's souls, wrapped together like a bubble of mist, floating freely, reflecting rainbows. This was before flesh, before bones crushed each other foolishly trying to join mortal bodies, before the outline of skin shielded us from one another. We both knew this, that we came from the same place, that we were joined in a place so uncommon that this world, which bound and confined us, could not understand the bond that flesh frustrated.

We became intimate friends again, desperate friends. This time she ached for me when I pranced by with the boy from Alabama. She began to love me. I hadn't stopped loving her, years will pass, this love will not cease.

I thought writing this years later would release me from her. But I feel no reprieve. Not yet. Maybe the only resolution is in the act of loving. Maybe I had to love her enough to let her go. I had to begin to love her more than I loved my selfishness. I disavowed what I had to do, I wasn't ready. I cried.

We became enraptured, entrapped, addicted to each other's eroticism. A kiss on the cheek inflamed me for hours. I witnessed her greed. Teasing reached new heights. Could I let go of my addiction to her, to her words? Would I let go? The desire to desire her — my weakness. I didn't care. I risked inviting her to my home every day, despite the moodiness she provoked. Her boyfriend grew more threatened each time I appeared. His hostility sharpened. Mine became silent when she approached. She and I, trapped in social circumstances. Propriety kept us apart.

Some women exude sex simultaneously with erotic movements. She was such a woman. Her scent alone emitted sensuality. I learned how boys had damaged her. I judged her damage. She punished me when I refused to continue the pattern with which she was so familiar. When I denied her the fight she sought, she would finally look elsewhere. So accustomed to brutality, she chose the victim's role. We sensed that dynamic in each other. The young woman held that if the games didn't work the first time, eventually I would play. I couldn't resist her when she agonized. After rushing to him, he would oblige by hurting her, then she would come to me. I rescued her, then resented my duty. And so we played this deceitful game, angry because we didn't know how to quit. I would spit fierce words at her. Sometimes, without uttering a sound, I hurt her. I manipulated just as she did.

Whatever bound us transcended friendship. And through our games I recognized when she would leave me again; each time she would go a little longer. She returned to him, the boy with the strong brown back. Almost facing him on the path that routinely led me to her, patrolling motionless from the street. The fog, the dull sky, the cold air warned me. He opened the door I had opened so often. I couldn't cry. I stood, the numbed observer. Long before he traced my steps to her door, I knew. I knew it was over again. She was tired of repeating our patterns. I was tired of her lies. I listened when the young woman lied to him on the telephone while I sat on her bed. Only now did I hear the lies were for me. I wanted truth, but I believed her lies because I believed my heart.

I refused to say good-bye. It's far better not to suspect when something is over. It's far better not to imprint that image permanently in one's mind. I prefer to march through the habits of the day treating good-bye as if it were not that at all, as if tomorrow we'll meet again for coffee. I began to mourn her. I don't know when I said good-bye, but I anticipated the moment. And it happened. The image marked in a memory I shielded from myself for years. I had to forget that predetermined second. So much more is stamped in my mind — her smile, her breath, her persistence. She wore me out. I needed rest.

❏

We picked cotton. My mother, sisters, brother, aunts, cousins, my grandmother. We would pick rows and rows of white-beige fiber with brown seeds embedded in its fluff. Picking fast, grabbing handfuls with fingers, often pricking them with spiny, sharp, leaves that hugged the plant's flower. Fingers bled from cuts, shedding red stains on the white balls. Sometimes wasps made their homes in the bushes and attacked anyone who disrupted their nests.

En la pisca, I followed my mother. I leaned over, picking quickly behind her. At dawn when we arrived in the field, I picked fast but soon lost her to a swift pace. By noon when we'd break for lunch, she would help me finish my row to work beside her after lunch again. She was a young woman then, younger than I am now. Young and resilient. Together, my mother, sisters, brother and I made the money we needed for school. I remember we were poor; poverty, it seemed, led us through those cotton fields.

In the fields, the women wore *gorras*, home-made bonnets to protect heads from scorching sun that baked our hands. Our bodies sweltered in the sun's heat through thin cotton dresses. Cool breezes would not relieve us until early afternoon when gusts teased the skin. Dusk was our time-clock. We weighed the *morrales*. The heavy sacks were heaved on scales to measure the cotton harvested and money earned. Ten cents a pound. One-hundred pounds. Ten dollars. A twelve hour day.

My brother and I filled burlap sacks, one-fourth the size of my mother's. I'd stuff mine full, he'd leave his half-empty but at the end of the week, we'd earn the same dollar for a week's wages. I resented his pact with my mother but it didn't matter. We all earned the same money for school clothes, number two pencils, and Indian Chief tablets.

An August morning, my forehead blistered, the nape of my neck dripped with sweat. I told my mother; she sent me to the *carpa*, next to the truck. My grandmother peered disapprovingly. Her eyes accused me of being lazy, too frail to be useful in the fields.

My mother had told me stories about *el wes*, traveling west to follow seasonal crops she and her family gathered. West to Arizona, I suppose. She wasn't sure. A young girl of eight, *en la pisca*, beside her mother daily. Her mother would instruct her to return to the *carpa* to start the evening's meal. The family lived in a tent while they worked the fields. She'd light bunson burners, a camper's stove, scoop flour from large bins, pour it into a big bowl and heat water from bottles until it was *tibia*, warm enough to add to the flour and manteca mix, preparing masa for tortillas. She told me she did little. Knew little. Eight years old, I thought. *Piscando algodón*. Cooking. Working like an adult and she worried that she did nothing. When did she play like a child, I wondered.

Sometimes she'd stay in the *carpa* to guard babies while the women and men picked. A newborn would cry and my mother would scamper to the field to find a hungry child's mother.

I wasn't aware of these stories when I lay on a foam mattress that morning. I was eight, I wanted to jump on trailers piled high with spongy, white cotton. Instead I cringed with stomach pains. My *güelita* scorned my frailty, my mother coddled me. Maybe she didn't want my childhood to be as short as hers had been. That morning, the sun and my grandmother's eyes scathed through me.

We picked cotton for Mr. Green. He owned huge fertile fields, hiring Mexicans who traveled north from Mexico and those who lived in nearby *pueblitos*. We lived in town, not far from his farm. He liked my mother. He would hire her, her sisters, her mother. Daughters joined mothers, working side by side, talking and joking for hours.

Mr. Green, a tall, lanky Anglo farmer, wore blue jean *petcheras* and a beige felt hat with a sweat ring around the band. I sensed in his gaze pity for Mexicans who worked his fields. I sensed he believed this was all we could do, labor in the fields like burros; mules, senseless and dumb. He was not unlike Anglo teachers. They'd glare at my brother and me, anomalies in the white school, mutes and mutants, for our silences, for our brown skin.

"Greezers," announced Anglo field hands when we slid past, leaning forward, pulling *morales* to be weighed. They would jeer at my aunts and sisters, mumble to each other, then snicker loudly. Later, in town, the same white workers heckle insults. They lean against a pick-up truck, one hand in a pocket, the other cradling a long-neck beer. "Hey, Meskin, where's your seester?" they mocked. Shamefaced, I focus on sidewalk cracks in front of the five and dime, run in, buy an almond Hershey's bar with the nickel my father had placed in my callused hand. In the fields, I savor the taste of chocolate, anxious for the day to end. Rushing past the Anglos drinking beer, I bite into chalk melting in my mouth.

We had earned most of our summer money when the brisk winds arrived, ruining the remains of the harvest.

"*Va llegar un chubasco,*" my father announced his weather report the night before the hurricane.

Teasing, my mother answered, "*Para ti, siempre va llegar una lluvia o el norte or lo que sea.*"

"*Vas a ver. No deben de ir a la pisca mañana.*"

My mother loved cool winds *el norte* released on afternoons when the sun exhausted us. We would arrive in the field early morning, sweating from sticky humidity. By afternoon, clouds gathered, covering the sun. Gusty breezes cooled us. Rain fell like huge pellets forming round circles on shirtsleeves.

This day, calmness falls like a warning. Silent clouds move rapidly like a high speed motion picture. My mother, bending over a row, darting up, peers into a dark, indigo sky. Her brow is wrinkled. Light rains had never kept us from picking, welcoming the wetness that moistened the musty cotton balls. Today, the air paused, took a deep breath, and frightened my mother. A sharp gust sweeps her blue skirt. The red scarf which held down her hat becomes undone. The home-made *gorra* tumbled through rows and rows. My brother and I chase it, his foot stomps on the brim. Harder rain pours. We can't see in front of us. The winds whip our clothes, bend tree branches. My brother searches the fields for my mother and sisters, takes my hand, we follow blurred movements leading to a rusted Chevy truck. Five of us pile in front. My aunt starts the engine; my brother and I shift on *güelita's* and *mamá's* laps. In the truck's bed, my sisters and cousins cover their heads making a tent from a blanket. I look over *mamá's* shoulder through the truck's rectangular back window, envying sisters and cousins who scream jubilantly as the vehicle dips and jumps through pot-holes.

The hurricane reached us in the morning. I studied gray sky from my bedroom window. I loved rain, but *el chubasco* was more exciting than anything I'd ever lived. It was Friday, the last day of August. Torrents of water clicked loudly, sporadically, against glass. There was no rhythm to the rainfall. Gusts of wind and rain smashed against windows. I waited, anticipating shattered glass. It was as if something ignited, as if something changed before me, and I thirsted for the change.

Sunday morning we woke to a flooded living room. An inch of water covered the wooden floor. My mother mopped quickly, hand-wringing a mop in a patched, red bucket; my sisters and I soaked towels under our feet, swishing back and forth through puddles. At the kitchen's back door, leading to a storage room, stood my father. In a wringer washer, he'd roll drenched towels, passing dry rags to our assembly line through a living room, kitchen, and back to him. With hands folded under his arms, eyes glazed over, my brother lingered in the hallway, pleased we couldn't return to the fields.

Calmness overshadowed the ruin left behind by *el chubasco*.

She practiced deception. So precise, her game, that even she was unaware of her lies. The young woman plotted deceit so exquisitely, deceiving herself, her lovers, her men. And me. But I refused the truth. I refused to listen for discrepancies in her stories. I consciously ignored misconstrued facts.

She tested herself. The young woman visited past her usual hour one evening. She liked to drop in after school. Often when she came by, the boy from Alabama would also show up. As soon as he entered the living room, she nodded, greeting him politely, then left, assuming I chose him over her. This afternoon she stayed. Maybe to prove something to herself. As evening drew near, she grew quieter. She experimented with the moment, with herself. He suggested our usual evening drive. On our way, we could drop her home. She consented.

The young woman settled in the back seat of his powder blue Impala. I squeezed in the bucket seat next to him. He asked for directions to her home. I didn't answer, coercing her to speak, her accent sounded melodic, yet blunt, her voice quiet. Not hearing her, he asked again. She spoke louder. Round, accented, vowels floated inside the Chevy Impala. I can't guess why I enjoyed listening to Spanish sounds maim English, but I did.

Dreams of her continue. They remind me of her back, her mouth, her touch. They brought me back home, but not to find her, to recover something I had witnessed that summer.

A dark sea mesmerizes me. I'm on a pier under the star lit sky spying visions that will torment. On the school yard, a boy, older than I, chasing me through hallways. In the cafeteria, nearby, he mimicked the rhythm of my arms, the tempo of my movements. The boy repeated phrases I spoke to someone next to me, his friends would snicker, he and his friends speaking sexual secrets, reveling in what they understood at fifteen. I was nine, an innocent nine. I grew to hate him.

In movie theaters, alone, on Saturday and Sunday afternoons, films saved me from languid summer days. Cool, dark, and safe, I escaped to someone else's passions. Often, I stayed for the same film, two or three times, waiting for a breathtaking heroine to appear. Two lover's would kiss. I pretended to know how lips felt.

I hear his voice two rows behind me. He grumbles in that same irritating tone, a tone filled with sexual insolence. He whispers my name. I ignore him. Again, he calls. A cold wave sweeps through me. I want to vanish, my refuge invaded by him. If I race home, he and his friends will follow. I hear my name. I hear his voice. I hear frightening murmurs. Finally, I turn.

"Leave me alone," I mutter.

But refusal was his invitation. I was his. I spoke. I spoke to him. He had a shred of me. He claimed me. His friends giggled, smacking their lips loudly like mock kisses. When my brother appeared in the darkness, I was relieved, but the mimicry at school continued until his family left town to follow seasonal work. I complained to my mother, to my friends Josie and Susie, but no one listened. A harmless young boy liked me.

"Just ignore him. What are you afraid of?" They each would give advice.

I am only nine, I wanted to scream. I am only nine and already my body lies to me. My breasts were newly formed. I wore a bra. The child in me was not prepared to greet a boy like him, but the child had abandoned me years before the days I feared at school.

A spring day invited muggy heat. I'm awake. Dew scattered droplets on a rusty window screen. Outside, the wrens that woke me sing. Stumbling, I bump into my brother. Through a bathroom door, my father shaves his face. I lean against the wall. I doze. Pangs of hunger force gurgles in my stomach, burying last night's dream. When pain jolts through me, I double over, arms across my abdomen.

"What's wrong?" my brother asks.

I look up with arms protecting a burning stomach.

"Stomach hurts." I'm barely audible.

"Huh?"

"Stomach hurts." I repeat softly.

"Oh." He traipses to the bedroom we share.

An ache persists. My father shaves in a small bathroom where too many damp towels hang on a single, loose rack, a rack falling from so much pressure. Shutting the door after him, I fall to my knees. White liquid with lime saliva and pieces of red apple splatter in the toilet bowl. Hovering over the porcelain bowl, I wait. Only red apple shreds float before me. Sweat drips down my forehead. I wipe my face, brush my teeth, urinate, flush yellow piss and green saliva. The sharp pain subsides. I dress. At the kitchen table, I eat three pancakes with butter and syrup. The food will not satisfy. I pick at my brother's leftovers; I swallow whole Oreo cookies from a brown, wrinkled lunch bag.

At lunch, a ham sandwich, potato chips, apple, nothing fills me. In my mother's house I smell flour sizzling in butter for thick gravy. Mashed potatoes, roast beef, Lima beans, home-made bread, and iced tea stretch a swollen stomach. I wash dishes, privately licking the pot of potatoes, rubbing the sides with fresh, warm, bread, savoring white dip. In bed, no longer hungry, I crave that which I cannot imagine.

In the morning, more false hunger wakes me, more chirping birds annoy me. In the bathroom, my father shaves. My brother silently passes me in the hallway. I'm doubled over. My father has not finished smoothing his face. I race to the toilet, vomit. Traces of food from the day before rise to the top of the bowl. A foamy brown substance covers particles of meat, bread, and vomit. I wipe my face with a stale towel. Beads roll down my waist and navel to pubic hair. For months, soft curls have begun to poke through underwear. I've wanted to shave, assuming I shouldn't. But, in the night once, I snuck a razor into bed to slice tender skin, leaving a scar. Now, my hair grows out prickly. This morning, sweat covers a wiry mesh; the growth repulses me. Moments later, after dressing, I'm hungry again.

I wear a frayed green and almost black, plaid dress with a droopy, white collar. No amount of starch could give life to the broad collar that lay flat against my neck. My older sisters had worn the same dress when it was not a faded green and gray. At the kitchen table, I gulp full bowls of oatmeal with sweet condensed milk, cinnamon and raisins. Grabbing a bag lunch my mother made, I peek inside. By fourth grade, my mother stopped making tortilla lunches for my brother and me. At school, I bite into pasty meat on white bread; anticipating dinner, I hope for fat, greasy, tacos and refried frijoles tasting of bacon.

Hungrily, for three days, I have eaten. I vomit all I eat. On the fourth day, in a class-

room, on the fifth row, I slump in my seat outside the circle where white students giggle,
playing word games. I observe them with
envy, but stomach cramps distract me from
their games. With permission slip in hand, I
tip-toe down a musty hallway, swing open a
wooden door scratched with graffiti. Red
sticky blotches cover the crotch of my underwear. With toilet paper, I wipe blood from the
cotton; I wipe blood from my outer labia. In
the bowl, between my legs, trickles of coral
color the water pink. Dissolving. It was as if
my body could not restrain itself, pleased to
continue its deception.

In slim purses, my sisters and cousins carried bulky paper pads; visible through their
underwear, held up with thin elastic garter
belts. They removed the blood stained pads,
folded and wrapped them with toilet paper,
stacking them neatly in bathroom garbage
baskets.

In the nurse's office, I doze on a table. She
takes my temperature. Cold aluminum
shocks my legs; spasms drive like knives
through my abdomen. The nurse hands me a
thick Kotex, sends me to the bathroom and
phones my home. Soon after, my father hovers in the hallway, worried.

"*¿Comó te sientes mija?*"

"*O.K. papi.*"

We drove home in silence. At dinner, I
couldn't eat my mother's cheese enchiladas.

From my room, as I glimpsed the evening's first star, I heard my sisters' murmurs, then bursts of laughter; dishes clanged against the sink. Faint noises lulled me to sleep.

I'm drawn to piers. Motionless, my legs fixed on wooden planks, I listen to waves, the surf, seagulls. It's here where childhood horrors like submerged riddles will unravel. The mysteries are buried somewhere inside me, but I can never remember everything, only frames flash before me, frames of unfamiliar scenes. This thing that hid from me, it would release the young woman from the coastal Texas town who followed me everywhere.

Before I met her I led a childhood filled with grim illusions and stomach-aches. Before the fourth grade, as young as eight, I suffered stomach pains. My mother took me to the doctor we couldn't afford. We trudged down a common road, pebbles crackling under our feet, accenting our silence. She held my child's hand in hers. The office was decorated white; white, antiseptic walls, a white, dull nurse. The Anglo receptionist asked my mother to write a name, an address, to fill a form with questions. My mother, embarrassed, handed back the pencil and paper, humbly asking her to scribble the answers. The telephone receptionist snatched the tools.

Her gesture screamed conceit. In fresh cotton dresses, she had sat in rooms where Anglo teachers encouraged her to articulate sounds, while my mother bent over fields of cotton in suffocating dresses that smelled burnt from the sun's heat. The receptionist judged my mother who had begged her mother to let her go to classrooms, where, she would be bigger and older than the children who ridiculed her size and color.

In a starched uniform, the nurse led us into a sterile room. She took my temperature. A gray-haired man, the doctor, kneaded me with icy, large hands. He pushed in my stomach groping for answers to my ailments, handed my mother a cup. I had to piss into the cup, but humiliation kept me from pissing. Finally, my mother ran the faucet in the sink. No one explained to me or to my mother why I had to do this, we just followed orders, fearing them and all they could do.

Their ways, their prerogative, followed us beyond sterile offices across the railroad tracks, causing stomach-aches that continue today. The gray-haired doctor hoped to cure me with little pink and yellow pills that I chewed like candy. Each night, before bed, my father reminded me to swallow the sweet medicine that coated my tongue with pink and yellow splotches.

On the pier, the sea is so dark it seems invisible, unseen. A black sky is illuminated with stars; delicate, bright survivors, dead, yet shining, light years later. I imagined myself floating above waves, like a survivor transcending depths. The water pulls at me, but I have more to consider, to resolve, before I move on.

She regretted her openness with me, speaking freely, exposing secrets she hadn't gleaned until they spilled out. I, too, regretted how much I hadn't left unsaid.

I saw her everywhere. Every woman I met owned something of hers; each of these lovers gave me the gift of her thighs, her stomach, her womb. I discovered her in everyone who came after.

Although I returned, I was convinced I hadn't come back to find her. I repeated to myself how I wasn't here for her, not anymore. After I left, she swept through me each time the breezes picked up the scent of honeysuckle. We had sucked the flower's tips to share a sweet drop that satisfied our tongues. We had shared this nectar. I would fight to keep distance.

I hadn't forgotten why I'd left. I instigated suicide with cheap wine and diet pills. When the pills weren't enough, I used needles, melting amphetamines with matches on stainless steel spoons, shooting the liquid into a blue vein. My heart would pound rapidly through my throat to my brain. I was in love with speed. I became powerful, delusional and powerful, until my psychic illnesses, my paranoia seemed more potent than me. By dawn, when I needed sleep, bottles of sour wine quieted inner voices. But the voices became louder, stronger, harder to control. Even in sleep, voices gave me orders. They told me to leave, to leave her, to save myself.

For years, I was lonely. I couldn't avoid loneliness. When I had forgotten to remember her daily, I recreated moments. I would conjure up the turquoise dress she wore, the one that taunted me as she rocked her broad hips down a grassy hill. Faintly, a spark flickers, then fades.

❏

Her husband owned her, sapping her, wanting every piece of her, expecting what he'd had as a child. He held her frantically. His possession. Always within sight of him, she mirrored him back to him. He was her purpose.

When they were together in a crowd, he demanded the crowd's attention. To impress. He sought attention, especially from men. And while he did, he dismissed other's successes, his own superior. He worked harder than anyone, he would boast. No matter what job or skill, Pelón reminded others he had excelled in high school and in college. Claiming he was the expert, more competent than anyone, he would speak into air. He didn't converse. He lectured. Pelón was ordinary, the kind of ordinary who remakes himself with boasting words to exaggerate mediocre talent.

When I returned, she had been married almost ten years. She waited after I left to commit herself to a hypocrite's ceremony. In his world, her reality had dwindled to a house with an empty baby crib. She stood in the middle of her kitchen, gaping at her floor, absorbed in the linoleum's stain, a muddy, brown, stain in the same corner of the kitchen. For years she had tried chemicals of every brand and each year a new one was invented, she tried that one. But the floor covering only looked thinner and paler and the dirty film reminded her that her world was imperfect.

I had left without saying good-bye. And now, back in El Pueblo, the young woman wanted to show me how life with Pelón was perfect, but the ugly spot interfered with her plans. Others would ridicule her treaty with the kitchen linoleum, only I understood, at least, sometimes, it seemed, I understood. Since I'd left, no one listened to the young woman's cries or anger. And no one questioned what moved her, not even Pelón, her husband, could detect the sorrow in her tired body. He liked her to be skinny, he said. He didn't suspect that her frailty had only developed since they'd married. Before marriage, she had been sturdy with a young woman's full, hoop like hips. He assumed she purposely didn't gain weight, but for her, a skinny body encouraged slow death.

The night before I step on her porch, I sleep peacefully. I'm with her on sacred land — the desert — not yet invaded by billboards and outsiders. I follow her through red earth that smells like wet, clean soil after rain. Ginkgo cactus and slender limbs of ocotillo fill the landscape, fat shapely boulders face a blue sky; I stride slowly down a dusty path, kicking rocks with my boots, my hands in the back pockets of ripped, faded jeans. In the distance, she poses on a screened, white porch. Dust blows, picking up speed like tiny dirt tornadoes. I lose her profile. A tumbleweed blows in front of me. I peer into the distance, toward the porch. The dust settles, she re-emerges, dashing into the house. Moving closer, I climb steps, turn an unlatched doorknob, pause, then step through. We had lived on this land before, she and I.

On her front lawn, years later, my feet dutifully obey me, climbing steps, pausing, bending beneath arched doorways to find her.

Hundreds, thousands of times I spoke her name, silently, aloud, in a whisper. I gaze into a mirror at an aging face pronouncing her name clearly, succinctly. She is me, fused, even when we're apart. I couldn't look into my own eyes without her mirrored back. Self-consciously, I hesitated to speak other names aloud, my voice stumbling over hers. I refrained from speaking, not wanting to call someone else by her name. And so I kept silent.

The young woman declares proudly she is an atheist when she spots *la Virgen de Guadalupe* dangling from a chain around my neck. I mock her resolution reminding her she had been a good Catholic girl, reciting the "Act of Contrition" without a mistake, avowing it's magic. I ridicule her conviction, wondering if Pelón's coaxing could dissolve what twenty years of kneeling at an alter to pray Hail Mary's had drilled into her. She defied old rituals, had become a non-believer.

I didn't challenge this thing that worked for her. She hadn't thought about it. Not really.

Her responses mimicked his and I understood their union, how she wrapped herself up in him. His every syllable over-shadowed her conversations. I had been with her in the same way when we were young, like that day under the tree, she stated resolutely she couldn't distinguish where she began and where I ended.

In a corner of the kitchen our hands hold fingers, playing a game, threading in and out, across the table. I feel strong. With her, I have courage.

To recognize truth is not easy when one is so close to home. To speak truth is even harder. Far from home, I am aware of myself. Guiding eyes around the room, in El Pueblo, I annulled the years I'd spent trying to forget. A closed door, opened. Excavating, digging deeper, like an archaeologist uncovering remnants, piecing together what she has only imagined for years.

Pleased to be with her, I speak about a future, one in which I and the young woman from El Pueblo live alone, away from her gluttonous husband, her hollow baby crib, this infertile life. I want her with me. I will have her with me. She pours a cup of coffee. I am rescuing her. To a desert. We will rest. Rest in peace.

He shatters my dream. It is a death dream. He stalks through the door like a rupture. Impetuous, he accuses me — the intruder — with glaring eyes. He comes to spy, pretending to be casual, friendly. The familiar scene jolts me to another time. She and I, belonging, thriving, in ways he would never fathom. He's in the room. Again. To ruin fragile trust. I never imagined she would revel in his lies to himself. She overlooked his arrogance, his narcissistic harangue. His charm, she said, appealed to her.

His was a formula. I measured the value, the simplicity of formulas. An outline simplified one's life, something to follow, step by step, hypothesizing the outcome. But blueprints that scientifically sketched out life's reason disillusioned me. I didn't want to deduce an outcome anymore.

I wondered, did she have spontaneity with him? Did he ever take her in the kitchen, spreading her across the table lunging a tongue between her thighs. She confessed to me often that she savored the soft organ's swift, electric, teasing movements on her stomach's flesh, gradually moving lower and lower, until direct contact and she shuddered.

The young woman unveiled this hunger as we'd lie on twin beds. Our first year in junior

college, she came to me on Friday nights. We
reported the week's events and the evening's
back seat brawl with some nameless boy. She
confessed details, delightfully. She told me
how she shook with pleasure from the strokes
of a ravenous tongue. I listened, opening to
her seductive words, wanting more particu-
lars to bond us intimately.

Intimacies of the flesh achieved through
words. That was our affair. Years later, I redis-
covered my compulsion to consummate intimacy through dialogue — to make love with a
tongue that spewed desire, that pleaded for
more words, acid droplets on my skin. With
her, I learned to make love to women without
a touch. I craved intimate, erotic dialogue. I
was addicted to words and she had spawned
the addiction.

We looked forward to these nights. She
slept on the bed next to mine. Sometimes I
would wake at dawn, drenched in sweat, a
flash of heat swept through me, then nothing.
I study her. Skin so tan, eyelashes black, the
lunar on her neck even blacker. A small dot, a
passion mark to melt my patience. She slept
peacefully. Satisfied to guard her, she shared
the boundaries of her body with me and no
one else. On those nights, she belonged to me.
That year, she belonged to me. She hadn't before. Not like this. We reached new intimacies,
beyond high school when we delighted in ad-
dictive passion. We did not repress the lan-

guage of this fixation. Our boyfriends, confused and angry, left us to each other. Finally, only each other, seduced by tempting words.

That year, watching her sleep fulfilled me. But later, my body would ache for more as I saw her dodge her own truth.

Once again, he would come between us.

I stayed through that first boy, the one with the beautiful brown back who picked rows and rows of silky, coastal cotton. I held her close, wiped her tears. He had left her for another girl with bigger breasts, her trophies at adolescence. Effortlessly, D-cup girls snared most high school boys. Prancing in a tight, low cut sweater, Mary Jane exhibited her trophies, preparing to plunge them in the face of her next victor. She singled out the boy with the beautiful brown back.

My young woman cries in my arms. He'd lied; he'd been with Mary Jane. But he accused the young woman. He was tired of me, he said to her. He wanted only her, "not some lezzy and a pet dog." Someone told me this, offering gossip in the contours of loyalty. The young woman wouldn't repeat his accusation, perhaps unconvinced that it was false.

I comfort her as she weeps, her head on my shoulder, I stroke her hair. Under my breath I call him names. *Desgraciado. Pinche puto.*

In junior college, our second year, she met him. Fall leaves draped sidewalks in orange and yellow. He appeared at our college with students from the university. A recruitment effort. President of the Mexican American Youth Organization, he wore the typical Pancho Villa, Emiliano Zapata mustache. Pelón, tall, mustached, with a gaunt frame. He moved like a cartoon, animated. The skinny pre-law major pushed himself in front of people transforming groups into audiences. His friends called him Pelón, a reminder that age would steal his wavy head of hair, a lion's mane. I observed him in the student lounge gathering recruits. An insecure womanizer, I thought, flirting with young men. I noted a sweet, effeminate gesture as he leaned forward placing his hand on a young man's shoulder.

"Make something of yourself. You owe it to yourselves, to your community." He shouted, spitting saliva, perhaps believing the louder he shouted, the more authority he earned. "Become a lawyer, an engineer." A crowd of young men interspersed with women listened, but his message was not for women. He preached to men, parading himself almost charismatically, unaware that he looked and sounded like an adolescent stumbling through clichés.

We lean against a wall, in a corner, half-aware of the crowd, acutely aware of him. His eyes are focused on a few men bumping shoulders against him. She breathes in my ear, ridiculing his scrawny shoulders, giggling about the bulge in his pants, wondering if "it" was also skinny. She reduces his virility to the thing men like him value — size, length, shape of penises.

She loved power. Illusive power. I rejected him from the beginning, refusing to notice how he drew her to him. In the corner of the room that day, she was mine. I refused to catch her eyes follow him. She prepared for him, a seductress who swayed a man's weakness for compelling hips.

To take from the source of someone to give to someone else, that is why she lured me. She took from me to be with him. But I offered her that. I envied him. The young woman had loved me, but my love wasn't enough. He had given her what I could not. Today, in her kitchen, years later, she admired my freedom from her choices, her panacea had worn off, a foundation crumbled beneath her.

After coffee and timid laughter, after his intrusion, I left. He comes through the kitchen door, throws me an indignant reproach, then fawns her. I rise to leave. He won again. She pretended she was unaware of our battle, looking after me for a promise that I would return soon. I answered with a furtive smile.

I wait, inventing a new purpose in El Pueblo before returning to her kitchen table. I don't seek her out, instead I visit places, childhood places.

My *güelita's* house. She's not watering the rose bushes or chasing chickens pecking her flower garden. After my grandfather died, she remarried a man my mother despised. The man she would never call step-father died from a heart attack in another woman's house, on her bed. Fifteen years with a strange man no one liked. My grandmother moved out from behind the railroad tracks into a nursing home, saddened at having buried two husbands.

Retracing steps to my parent's home, memories stream forth. The owners vacated the house after it burned in an electrical fire. My family had since moved but my cousin told me about the blaze. She and my aunt wandered through the remaining ashes to mourn what my family preferred to deny.

A filthy field lined the gravel road to *abuelita's* wooden house. The neighborhood dumping ground, covered with coffee grounds, lumps of cold lard that had fried too many corn tortillas, dried limbs of Christmas trees, mud-filled coke bottles too chipped to trade in for penny candy — the field confessed the neighbors' habits. Chicken carcasses and slippery rivers of *manteca* had been dumped over the fence that day.

Passing the cotton gin, I sidled behind the abandoned building, roaming along railroad tracks. My brother and I memorized each feature of this short cut. I mulled over how he had grown into a considerate, nondescript man with no apparent goals, yet, his life seemed appealingly prudent. He lived in his bedroom in my parent's house where he watched TV until two or three a.m. on nights when he didn't get up early for work. I comforted myself pretending he led a life beyond that room, outside that television.

On the railroad tracks, we were each other's confidantes. At age eight, I trusted no one more than I trusted my brother. We strayed through the back route, ignoring our father's fears, his warnings of danger. The main road, lengthy and dull, stretched along the ditch at the edge of town leading to my grandmother's, the same ditch my drunk grandfather drove his car into one Christmas eve. My grandfather in the ditch, sprawled on the ground at the *jamaica*, spoiling holidays, ruining school nights, these town stories about his drinking vividly spill forth.

My brother and I defied my father, balancing feet on tracks like high-wire acrobats, betting that whomever arrived at *güelita's* without falling off the steel rails won the game. I don't remember clearly, but this did happen. We took the back route home from my grandmother's, playing the same game, balancing and falling, balancing and falling. In the distance, a group of young boys approach us. They're my brother's age, ten or eleven, but bigger. Three, maybe four or five, they are a pack of dogs stalking, proving something, but only to each other. The biggest one blocks my path, grabs me, smothering my face with his, trying to kiss me. I fight, resisting brusque strength. The other boys follow, each takes his turn, suffocating me. I'm scuffling, slipping from hand to hand. They shove me. I fall. My brother stands helpless, trying not to cry. Finally, the wild pack disappears into faint, vertical lines in the distance, melding with the track, becoming the thread where we balanced and fell. I race home to safety, crying and wiping saliva from my face. His steps behind me, slow; his face, terrified. I wondered if he was capable of hunting with boys like that, attacking girls and silences. I didn't think so. He seemed molded by a softness, the softness that had made him my only friend, but at home, while I washed dishes, he watched TV, while I peeled potatoes, he watched TV, and when I grew up and left home, he watched TV.

At my grandmother's, I pause, glaring at the house next to hers, across the street. *La costurera's* home. I hadn't entered the town seamstress's house for years, avoiding it at childhood, but today, I gape across the dirt road at the yellow house, repulsed.

Gripping an armchair, in my room, I am shaken. A baby is two or three, maybe younger, but speaking. She is dressed in a primrose, ruffled dress, a dress to emphasize rosy cheeks. A young shapely woman in black heels, dark hair pulled back in a bun, wearing a white dress with black polka-dots, holds a child's moist hand; they are hiking to *la costurera's* a humid, spring afternoon. Child and mother resemble each other, especially upper lips, curved with peaks. Cars drive by at high speed, break, and back up. A driver asks the shapely woman if she and her daughter want a ride. She frowns, *"No, gracias."* They continue walking, a long walk. The baby is hot, the mother, crouched on bending knees, wipes the baby's face with an ironed, starched handkerchief. The beads of sweat vanish from a lip that curves and peaks like two slim mountains. The stiff handkerchief scratches the baby's skin.

La costurera sews for families too poor to shop for store clothes, designing Easter dresses from Sears' catalogue photos. *La costurera* with three sons, young boys, no husband, no father. That afternoon, *la costurera* and the mother compare colors and patterns.

Two sons take the baby's hand. She follows. In a bedroom, behind a bed, in a corner, they fondle her, they fondle a tiny girl beneath a primrose dress. Curious boys poke fingers beneath her underwear. An older brother stands at the doorway, guarding those who play harmless children's games. A boy pulls down his pants, holds a hard penis in his hand, rubs it against a baby girl's flesh. The baby's eyes track a thin, cinnamon cockroach slithering against a wall, it finds a crack and slips through an opening that was invisible, non-existent. She is numb. This numbness will inhibit her for years.

She would become a woman who craved mixed sensations, that which would never satisfy her, to not be satisfied was her satisfaction, chasing an unconscious memory. She would long for a stinging slap on tender skin. A soothing roughness.

In high school, the young woman from El Pueblo blurted out how her step-father groped her young girl's breasts for years. As she grew older, her muscular boyfriend warded off the step-father who had fondled her when her mother was at work. He began when she was a little girl, eight or nine. When we met, she was already well-rehearsed at sex. Humiliated when she told me, I denied what I already judged. Boys, cousins, uncles had pawed me. No one suspected. I wanted to tell her. But I didn't. I let her talk to me about how she anesthetized herself for years while I invented another childhood for myself with silence. She began to suspect something was wrong or peculiar about me and when she decided I had betrayed her, she deceived me with ease. I had restricted my nightmares to the privacy of my bedroom, she bravely announced hers without censure.

Missing links began to mend this life's chain.

My grandmother's house, the railroad tracks, my brother, *la costurera's* sons. In sleep, they visit. They bring a disturbing vision of a little girl, a baby. She slides from a woman's canal. I reach for her fragile limbs. Those who shun the girl leave. I embrace her, cuddling her. My brother rejects the baby. I force her into his arms. She falls. Her head cracks loud against the floor. Quickly, I recover her. My father has been peering through the doorway. I hoped he hadn't seen me pick her up. I pretended I hadn't dropped her, that she wasn't hurt, but her half-shut eyes struggled for consciousness. She's fine, she's fine, I lied to myself. I lied to the child. A train's shrill in the distance reminds me I may flee, take the child with me, somewhere safe, far away. I wake up. The train thundering, a thunder that could shatter glass, wakes me.

In El Pueblo, I reconstructed this childhood.

The young woman left me shortly after meeting Pelón. Fall kept me busy. Another year to reflect on what I didn't understand.

She wanted to wound me. I cried for her touch, any touch. How much longer would I return for moments doled out like flawed jewels. I recreated her greed, listening in my head to words she spoke, that she was in love. The words, like abuse. The young woman would speak to muster reaction. I said nothing. She spoke another way, wondering out loud, asking why he hadn't called. My silence only urged her to berate me more.

We repressed honesty, reserving it for someone else, something else, just as in high school, when she went back and forth between her boyfriend and me, we repeated this pattern. And again, when Pelón would insult her, she'd hurry to me but not for comfort. The young woman needed assurance that I was like him, that I would also punish her, believing she deserved punishment. But we hurt each other more than we had before. In college, we began a savage game. I hit her, tightening my grip around her arm, bruising the skin, leaving purple blotches. I wanted to clutch her, to own her. I could only reach her with cruelty. She looked at me as if she didn't recognize me. She became crazed like me.

Crying, she came to my room late. Another argument with Pelón. I had fallen asleep. Her knock didn't startle me. I expected her.

They argued about plans, to be with or without each other. He would graduate in the spring, go to law school, but before law school, he wanted to marry, each would help the other through school. She resisted. They argued throughout the year. He threatened her. He threatened to leave her, he threatened to marry someone else, he threatened her with his fist.

I kissed the bruise on her arm. She pulled back, angry at him, fighting me. I listened to her anger, the fury in her voice frightened me, and as she raised it, her outrage terrified me more. Shoving me, she accused me, shouting that I was weak, that only he loved her. Her words land like a slap. I whimper, "I've loved you longer than anyone. More, than he ever can."

I compound her purple marks. She is satisfied to hate me. I couldn't stop. Nor could she. The young woman expected this, as I did. Her face twitches, her words snarl. Puckering thin lips, squinting oval eyes, she narrates scenes that strike like blows. Spilling portions of sexual technique, forcing me to listen. Less and less, I trust her, yet she'd done this so many times, provoking jealousy, always, always, inciting rage.

We rehearsed this same drama. She would come to my room. Drunk. Reclining, cross-legged on my bed, I listen to lust. She fuses pain with pleasure. His was a violent passion. Mine was an unnamed urgency.

In the dorm hallway, I swerve to avoid erupting anger, although she hasn't touched me, her hands choke my neck. The young woman paralyzes me, then attacks. It was, I'm sure, her pleasure.

The day he recruited students for the university, his words were big, his message mindless, mimicking phrases of genius he'd read, but none came from the core of him. He had no personal style, no gift to create from the root of himself. He threw up other's words, not his own.

Snubbing me, he sensed I didn't worship him. Pelón condemned me, always spurning who I was, what I did, and what I meant to her. He told friends and strangers I was a sell-out, "una vendida," he'd call me and anyone who didn't bow to him, rumoring I wasted time with queers.

I enjoyed how I threatened him.

❏

Those years at the university, I found reprieve with Juan. The chocolate-skinned artist wore a Zapatista mustache, his features carica-tured. Shaped by suffering, he bore the past, unafraid to admit his nightmares. Juan didn't take from you to deceive later. Humbly, he ex-pressed himself with a body scarred and a memory wounded from horrors in Vietnam.

I met Juan through friends, mutual Anglo acquaintances match-making two odd, mis-placed objects from their collection. I was at-tracted to his quiet voice, his silences, a man secure with himself. Juan was an intuitive painter, not an amateur as one would assume for a twenty year old. His painting had hung in a New York gallery, "a young artist series," he told me. A high school teacher recognized talent and entered a national contest with his 12 by 12 inch canvass of stray dogs, cobalt — against an indigo sky. Two angular dogs, tails alert, howling at an orange half-moon, toured the country. He told me one day, in a park, on his blue blanket, clothed in his blue shirt and blue jeans, smoking menthol cigarettes. Softly, the words posed in air, he paused as if eyeing them just slightly above his head, unfurling. Juan did not boast his genius. That was not his need.

He wept easily, tears streaming down fleshy cheekbones shined like crystals. Shrapnel scars on his tanned stomach stirred his nightmares, causing him to weep. He had been one of thousands; the poor, brown-skinned boys who could not protest the war in college class rooms. No one had prepared Juan for college. No one warned him about war.

In a friend's apartment, we lie on a worn mattress, wire springs poke through the sheets. He pulls off his shirt, then my blouse, the gesture, like a contract. Palms smooth over skin gently. Juan's chocolate chest is a marred topographical map, finger lakes and rivers branch from a main line, trickling through muscles. As I kiss each rupture of flesh, wanting to heal that which I cannot touch, I fall in love with his map, tracing paths with an index finger, I move the finger to my mouth, then rub spit like salve on lesions. I fall in love with chestnut eyes, and a rare, cynical smile.

We will become companions who do not understand why they have survived, with nothing left to offer.

Lying on his back, Juan sketches a story. Dispassionate, unmoved, he talks about a black, star-less night when sparks flew and a moon didn't guide him through trenches. An warmth oozed from his stomach. He pressed fingers against his stomach, bringing them to his nose and mouth, he smells and tastes an unfamiliar stickiness.

"I thought it was a dream," he said as we lie on a mattress covered with a maroon tie-died sheet.

He awoke on a hospital bed where a nurse wrapped his bandages and a doctor sent him back to muddy ditches, his home. He fell to more fire, but his time was up and he returned to a place that hated his brown skin. I wanted to ask questions, to probe, but his shyness kept me from intruding. I had read about men who raped Vietnamese girls as routinely as they shaved their beards. Rape was commonplace for them, almost a daily chore. I wanted to ask if he was like them, or if he'd hung out with men like that. I didn't think he was capable of hurting women, of abusing war's license to brutalize females and expel men's fears.

In motel rooms, we made love, as if only he and I were alive, but when I escaped rooms where the smell of our heat shrouded air, I forgot him, suspending the imprint of his fingers on my back; memories didn't follow me beyond rooms where we shared transient love.

Before our final meeting, I left. Years would pass before we bumped into each other again, thrown together briefly, we ran into one another in the same neighborhood of the same friends who had introduced us. He invited me home, cooked for me, led me to bed, but we both sensed emptiness born from years of waiting, years of doubt. Letting go of illusion was easy after that.

The first time I left wasn't as easy. We drove to the beach at midnight to play in a phosphorescent lime-green color that creatures infused in Gulf waters late summer. He flung a sparkling T-shirt on the sand. Warm waves gushed over naked breasts. His arms, wrapped around my waist, kept me from falling into the undercurrent. The moon shone on a single dark figure in the ocean, clutching; the way he clung frightened me. When he drove us home in my burgundy Chevy, I leaned on him, assured by his chest, its resounding depth.

The next day, I found his boots in the back seat, damp and sandy. By the time I delivered them to his front door, I had decided not to tell him I was leaving. I didn't knock on the door.

I placed the boots on the front porch and quickly drove away without uttering good-bye.

I talk about him to remind myself about the differences. The different ways I loved men from women. The way I forgot him so easily disturbed me. He quickly became a muted memory, like all other men, their bodies unclear to me. But her body and the women who came after her spoke lucidly to me. Women's breasts alone were unforgettable, sumptuous, silky, like words whispered to soften flesh. With him, I remember a chocolate-skinned chest marred with its unique beauty.

❑

Driving through the high desert of the Southwest, I left home. My memories flowed as quickly as the landscape passing in my rear view mirror. In the mirror, I sighted Shiprock floating, surrounded by nebulous clouds, solid, massive, yet gliding silently. Natives named the rock formation centuries before Spanish ships arrived hundreds of miles west or southeast on the continent's shores. The Navajo fixed their destiny and named the "winged rock," as if prophesying a wish to flee from danger. Somehow linked to that past, I glanced back at the sculpted boulder. Trying not to lose control of the wheel, I looked ahead, but the road's white line moved rapidly, dizzying me. When I lifted my eyes to squint in the mirror, Shiprock steadied me, reminding me I could return to the high plateau if I ever finished searching.

I fled the Gulf coast to Los Angeles, driving through this northern desert. I didn't know I would be drawn again and again to red mounds of earth and rose colored rocks. Something summoned me, but I drove on.

Free from her, I had escaped El Pueblo. In those years, there were many women, many lovers, many nights when lust thrilled me in ways she never had. Each lover sedated me with kisses and promises that lasted through the night, through the month, even through years.

There were men too. Men who stimulated for an afternoon and asked for nothing more. Men who elicited hard sex. No ties or fondness. No kisses. Men with muscular, wide, chests, firm stomachs, and dark brown, expansive shoulders. Hands would firmly cup strong buttocks pounding and slipping on wet skin. A swollen, cock would push into a sleek cunt, jabbing slowly then faster, welcoming hard flesh. An athletic man lifted a woman's legs, anchoring them on his shoulders, stroking a prick to thicken it, then inching inside, nudging through dry tightness. A voice would scream, inviting pain.

I met them everywhere, in classes, at work, in supermarkets, in bars; some were friends, but never lovers. They served a purpose shortly after I renounced her, but none of them could touch my skin like her, rasping lightly, not even the women who satisfied me. Women after her offered what she never gave, but their stories won't fill these pages. Instead, her story suffocates me, anxious for resolution.

In that rural Texas town, repression conceived my wishes. To understand what you are doing while you're doing it is powerful, but self-betrayal has motivated me more; when I was nineteen, I didn't understand, but now, much later, ignorance can't comfort or deceive me.

Self-inflicted wounds marked me at an early age. At four, I chewed my fingernails. I won't repress the habit. I relish it still. I bite nails and peel back cuticles until I draw blood. Raw chewed skin covered with drying blood, fingers layered with scabs. My thumbs throb where the cuts separate the nail from the skin. With short sharp nails, I pick back thick cuticle skin. Blood oozes from my thin fingers. The blunt weapons will grow for a week, then, I chew the thumbnails and the middle fingers with my teeth, spitting out particles. I leave the forefinger on one hand long to cut skin. The faces are fat and stubby. Physical pain will test me, excite me even. At eight I learned to take a sharp razor cutting designs on the heels of my feet, roughly shaping triangles, squiggles. I hated my feet. Blood still cakes the callused skin. I peel back pale, thin calluses, then cut underneath exposing pink flesh. Scars brand my heels. I anesthetize myself with pain. Blood oozes from my hands and feet.

In a new home, I awoke to lust, hungering for contact, taking the nearest possibility, gratified briefly, then, the morning, the bright sun; a stranger in the light reminds you, you don't want familiarity. Just sex. Better to leave before morning when regrets are not so obvious.

Over and over, I said good-bye to her. With other lovers, I staged good-byes. How many women have I loved and run from because of her? How many times have I sunk so close to eyes, to skin, to touch, only to escape its nearness, its scrutiny. I began to live a life of guilt and vice. In dark bars where cigarettes unfurled smoke signals to the ceiling, I'd find women. I would lie on their beds lulled into peaceful sleep lovers discover after bodies explore textures. I kissed mouths skimming my hand past the arch of waists. Inside a woman's thigh, my fingers searched vaginal lips that spoke desire. I thrust fingers and silicone phalluses into moist vaginas, driving and shoving in and up to a spot that made a woman gasp into air, into longing. Warm breath draws me closer to a face.

I enjoyed strangers' bodies, savoring the excitement of anonymity. Much later, when emptiness was all I would find, I caught myself. Repulsed. I couldn't remember names or faces; only shabby bars, loud disco, or the blue MG I drove came to mind. The two-seater drew women to the passenger seat to ride through the Hollywood hills and southern California cold beaches. We would meet once, maybe twice, then not again.

Daily, I'm reminded, I have no right to love as I love. I live in a place that ruptures and negates this practice. Don't misunderstand me, even when I'm told to hide from public, to meet only in unlit rooms where you can't see us, I'm defiant.

A baby goes for a walk. A mother walks her baby. Baby and mother walk down a used path on the side of a gravel road. They are walking to *la costurera's* house.

This can't be explained. In shadowy rooms are groping hands. You beg, you beg silently, but groping hands in the darkness won't quit what you yourself a child don't know how to end.

This is betrayal I've been speaking about.

Everyday this, my past, reminds me I've been vulnerable, too vulnerable. I hand out weaknesses strangers measure. These childhood fears are triggers discharging messages, "don't move," "wait." I am inhibited by memories.

I'm brooding in a meeting. Confessing. Healing. Forgiveness was once impossible. In the meeting people gather to release transgressions. We speak words and as they mingle in mid-air, grief dissolves. Infused with air, injuries evaporate. Tears stream down my face. The woman sitting across the room has blond-brown strings of hair. Blond eyebrows with darker brown strands emphasize thickness over her light gray, almost blue eyes. Her skin is winter's pale tan. A slim nose and high cheek bones give her indigenous features. She glances at me, then looks away, maybe embarrassed by my tears. I guess she's attractive. I'm tempted to go to her, take her hand and press its warmth against my cheek. I wonder who she reminds me of? Someone. Doesn't matter.

The Trial

. . . tormented shadows haunt my dreams
as I sleep tormented at night.

The Hour of the Star
Clarice Lispector

What happens here, began long ago. The story began in a hot, steamy room where three boys groped a baby's body.

I read about the rape.

In a suburb of Los Angeles, I spread out on my kitchen table reading the morning newspaper. Alone. Drinking too many cups of espresso with warm milky foam, contemplating mountains layered with clouded, dirty film. A town whose name was not muttered outside the Gulf coast stirred chaotically when a woman didn't hide her rage, screaming for someone or something to help recapture her future; but those who said they sought truth distorted her words.

I read her name.

Ermila. Ermila.

I repeated the name in a soft breath, eyes scanning newsprint. The rapists' names

weren't familiar names. Four were aged sixteen to twenty-five. One was older. They were
on their way to a cock fight, to illegal gam-
bling in rural back roads. Drunk, ready to
pounce. They would each take a turn with
her. I imagined this. Saw them drive up in a
banged up beige Ford Galaxy, pull her in from
the side of the road where she strolled at dusk
to her *abuelita's*. Four men thrust her into
the back seat. The driver keeps the engine
running. I imagine her terror. They finish
raiding her, drive back to the road where they
found her, push her out of the back seat; she
rolls down an embankment, grassy, dry from
the day's heat. No one would view her lying in
a ditch. She regains consciousness, stands
up, fumbles with a ripped skirt and flees to
her grandmother's, her body aching.

Her bruises, internal, her skin unscathed, the
police would lie. She is scarred inner flesh.

Five men with boys' faces, boys' screams.

She would remember the faces and identify
each one. But there was one. A leader. The
loud one. She remembered him most of all.
Saw his face, heard his boasting voice in
nightmares. Her flesh deadened, could not respond to contact anymore. How do you recreate loving touch in memory when repulsion
ruptures the body, the psyche.

Ermila will have hallucinations, recurring nightmares about a woman trapped, swallowed by a reptilian creature wrapping itself around her waist, down to her feet. Her shoulders and head struggle, pushing and sliding, arms held down, crushed. A faceless animal will grip her. Writhing to free herself, lying on the ground straining, twirling her head, rolling her eyes to look at whomever stands behind her, she despairs, looking for help. She bellows a frightful cry. She sees a man, his face sadistic. The beast will devour her. The sadistic man savors how the monster will swallow her legs, her thighs, inching toward her waist. She can't escape.

Who would take the nightmare, have it for her every night so she could rest. When she fell asleep, she slumbered easily until visions would terrify her. She awoke, frightened, unaccustomed to spirits she hadn't befriended. Her eyes searched the room for the clock. One-thirty glowed in luminescent green. The time anchored her. After her slumber, she tossed miserably, waiting to slip away. Her arms jerked. Hour after hour, until five o'clock when morning light split a black sky, she battled like this, back and forth, distrusting dreams. She would struggle, keeping herself from tranquillity. At dawn, light soothed her. Only the dawn light would soothe her. No human touch would brush back dampened hair from a sweating forehead. No one wanted to caress her, but she didn't want to be caressed.

I called her again, the young woman from El Pueblo. Refusing to go back to her kitchen, we would meet in an open field not far from town. Driving slowly through a short main street with old brick buildings lining the paved road, a one-room library was next to a two story bank with a colonial facade of four columns. My brother and I would play among the columns, skipping and hiding, winding home after school. Summers, I would spend hours in the air-conditioned library, checking out books to entertain me on my twin bed until my mother called me to make iced tea or mash potatoes for dinner.

I drive until I reach deserted farm land. Immediately after she arrives in a clean black convertible, I disclose myself. I'm so eager to tempt her, to clutch her hands, grab her face. I tell her how I have to speak quickly, afraid I won't express everything I planned. I am telling her how the last time I saw her, not in her kitchen, but afterwards, at a party, she wouldn't meet my eyes.

"Instead, you just brushed against me, like you wanted to tease me."

I shake nervously, I'm short of breath, I want to say more, but you won't respond and so I pause, arguing with myself, not sure how much more I should say. I gaze at a sky so blue, I lose myself in its immaculate clarity. We sit quietly. You're afraid to speak. I'm reliving the party, eager to share with you how you taunted me.

You bounce in. I hide behind a crowd. Squeezing between bodies, I wave from across the room assuming you prefer comfortable distance, but you approach. We speak a few paragraphs, our fingers fumble lightly, accidentally, but we share nothing openly. You seem careful not to seize me with words. Instead, you speak carefully, cautiously. There are no enticements between us. You are somewhere else, with someone else. Only for split seconds, you are with me.

Privately, and in private, you're shy. So am I. Shy. I want to overcome shyness to meet you differently from who you pretend to be with me. I wait. But you offer no signs. Only a few side glances. You won't look into my eyes. No contact. No touch. Publicly, you're not so shy.

I've admired how you dance with women and men in crowded sultry rooms. Like this one. Sexily. Erotically. You dance. I want to dance with you. Fast. Faster. Then slow. I'll whisper in your ear when we dance slow. I'll whisper how I want my fist inside you. Sticky hardness, jabbing. The undaunted reality of fingers twisting, squirming inside you.

What would you answer if I whispered this in your ear? Would you smile, laugh as only you can, your laughter is the sign you offer. You used to giggle at things I said. Giddy, you'd hold back, then look away. You would become shy again, recognizing how I touched you in some familiar, ancient way.

At last, I speak. A warm breeze encourages honesty. I say how sometimes you still want me, but you won't say it. Not with words. With nuances. Occasionally, you slip. Like that night at the party. Your eyes lingered on my smooth brown neck, firm arms and shoulders, a curved waist. I wanted to ask if you'd studied my expressions. Do you see I look puzzled sometimes? Can you tell I'm not easily tamed? Like a wild animal, I demand time. Plenty of time. I insist on vigilant kindness. At first, you must approach slowly. With caution. I'll run if you come too close, too soon, too fast. When I discover your trust, you must grab me. Forcefully. Roughly. Take control. I'll turn myself over. I will. I've learned this about myself. How I need love.

"Will you ever have the courage to leave this place?" I break the silence again.

You have no answers. We stretch out on grass under a cottonwood tree like our first meeting. More than fifteen years have passed since the first moment I became so enthralled by you. You contemplate an azure sky with mobile clouds, eyes fixed on a cumulus cloud shaped like a soaring eagle, its wings outspread. A sudden breeze blows strands of your black hair back as if in flight. The tree's white, delicate balls of cotton blow in the breeze. A few stick to your hair. With my hand, I shake them off. You say nothing. You listen, expressionless. I continue my confession, hoping to change your mind, to win you back at least momentarily.

You come to the city alone, branded by his absence. I'm surprised you're there at all, at Ermila's fund-raiser. You wind into the room forcing courage with a smile. Outside of El Pueblo, Ermila's believers would collect contributions from sympathizers. College students, eager liberals, and paired women filled the living room of someone's house. Thrift store furniture — a ripped, black and red plaid couch and two scratched coffee tables with ring-shaped water stains were pushed against a wall. The ruined pine tables on each side of the couch are covered with paper cups and beer cans. Cats roam the rooms for an empty space to stretch.

You speak to someone. A man. You take a paper cup from him. Then, as if floating above me, you vibrate. I shudder. An amethyst light gleams around you, then disappears. You wear a color I've never seen you wear. You almost always wear black. I say you shine in rose hue. You're not so shy when I compliment you. You smile. You talk, animating words with gestures, hands sweeping air, you talk to someone. I walk away, but soon, you stand beside me. I sense you, vibrating like a steel magnet. You speak casually about clothes. I respond with what I think pleases you. You're pleased. But I don't know you anymore. These last years, I recreated you. And you, you're more suspicious of me than you've ever been. You can't grasp what I want from you.

In the open field, I deliver nothing more, echoing distrust in a lengthy, silent, moment. All I can do is recreate that night, how you acted, what I did and didn't do. I speak again to confess what I'm enduring at that moment under the tree, hoping you'll relive the past with me.

Someone from El Pueblo is surprised you're here. He asks you for Pelón. You grin at the suggestion that you're free tonight, that your presence is like betrayal to your husband. I walk away from the joking intimacy between you, but minutes later, I sense warmth. Incremental warmth. Here you are. Beside me. I forget I am alone with my need. I pretend you're beside me, that you want me that much. We listen to people around us. Mostly women. They interject phrases about Ermila's trial. Pelón's name is mentioned once or twice; you raise your eyebrow, concentrating, listening. I hear nothing. I focus on you, wondering if you're here to spy for him or if guilt has brought you to your husband's enemies.

We lean against a bookcase. Your arm grazes mine. A light touch. You take a pastry. A tangy lemon bar, asking if I want half. I respond yes, assessing your fingers twist the sweet cake. You place the piece in my hand. I eat it. Not hungrily. It doesn't satisfy. I want you more but can't say. I won't say. You start to leave. Say you need to go. I want to ask to go with you. I want to ask but don't. You prepare to leave. You don't say good-bye. I try to corner you. To say good-bye. You ignore me. Already, you've forgotten me in the room with you. Already, I'm not even a memory. This is how you forget me. This is how you are with me. One moment, you brush against my skin, then, you're gone without a word, and I'm left to wonder, when will she walk in the room again, how long will I wait while she decides who she is, what she wants.

That night, she comes. We talk. She lavishes me. I wake to vivid words, potent colors, shades of rose like desert earth to cleanse the heart. In the room, I smell her. The sweetly-sour perfume causes gagging. My stomach convulses. I want to exorcise the images. Every night, she reminds me she's not with me. Her angular face, her glossy black eyes come every night. In this other place, she intuits how much I miss her, how much I need her.

Eyes closed. I lie on my bed. Your arm's flesh skims mine. I relive the evening with you beside me against a bookcase. I turn my head to whisper to you. My breath warming your neck, pausing, I blow softly. You close your eyes. Keep them closed. I wonder, do you see him in your mind's eye? You're beside me, but you go to him. I don't make a move to change that. I prefer to beg for you. You know this, know you can't trust my evasive acts. You turn on me.

"Will you stay this time?" you ask, shifting on the grass beneath the tree.

"If you asked," I lie.

You hear the lie. Always have. You master me too well. You know, at this moment, I am aching for the perfect folds inside your skin. So you play. You'll continue to gamble. You don't want to stop. Like me you won't stop. We've never known how.

We leave the open field. Grass stains cover the seat of your threadbare jeans, the same jeans you wore those high school years. I remember when they were new. The first day you wore them, I jerked the belt loop prankishly to keep you from slipping away. You yanked your waist so hard I ripped a hole, tugging you. Today, your flesh peeks through the frayed hole. I haven't won her back, I thought, her hips swaying in front of me. Neither she nor I can capture what we want. We covet that which leaves us wanting more.

The ocean water gleams. The sun is setting. I'm shivering. Waves shine like silver, gliding, rhythmically peaking and dropping. I'm parked on a sand dune, glaring at the sunset's fiery burgundy over the water. In the field, you were cool, uncommitted. Your silences, full of him. When I searched your eyes, I saw him, not you. This is our familiar game, like chess. We distract each other with ordinary, threatening moves, then charge with what's unexpected. We've become predictable at a game never won, a game never over. Back and forth, one chases, the other runs. Running and chasing. Apprehensive. A runner stops. Someone in the distance turns to follow.

Like swift, cutting words your greed for him pricks me. I open to you again. Another way. With deception. I'm deceptive. I lie to you. I'm a liar proud of her lies. I admit my deception. I lied to my mother. I've lied to every woman I thought I loved and to every woman I know I loved, I lied even more. And men were never worth making up lies for, so I spoke unkind truths to them. But lies, always sweet, special deceit for women.

"No, I've never felt this way before."

"Yes, I'll stay forever."

Women want these falsehoods suspecting them as falsehoods yet denying they're lies, until later, then anger over stories they assumed were deceit all along. The time will come when I'll also prefer silences. I imagine telling her all this. I deceive myself, swearing she despairs.

I'm relieved to be alone these fitful nights. I don't fool myself. She won't leave Pelón, the man to whom she is more committed since the trial began. In the courtroom, his trial becomes hers.

❑

César Díaz, el Peloncito, was a man with devout opinions, true to himself and to men, unaware of how much he loathed women, yet he revealed himself daily when he described how women's words were never truths, only lies and fantasies. Slogans he had once sworn by, he repeated in the courtroom. Pelón defended the rapists, accusing a white media of framing innocent young men, making them a gang of barrio punks. He was so sure of himself that when he spoke about gringo enemies, he forgot who Ermila was and where she came from.

"And Ermila, what about Ermila?" I ask the young woman grabbing her arm through a crowd emptying the courtroom. Pelón hurries ahead, unaware I pull her back. She doesn't answer, searching nervously for Pelón outside on steps surrounded by reporters.

They tried to censor her anger. The compassion some offered was not compassion at all, but instead words meant to stifle her, to say, "Don't do this, Ermila, don't talk to the strangers. Why do you say these things? You make your life harder." These words came from women, *tías y vecinas*, only her *güelita* listened and repaired her broken flesh the night she stumbled in wailing at her abductors. "*Desgraciados*," Ermila shrieked.

Early evening, as dusk faltered between light and darkness, I looked for Ermila at her grandmother's. I drove along the gravel road, her path on the day she was abducted. A two room house stood alone at the end of a road where chickens paraded through a garden of tall rose bushes, scratching a bed of violet petunias whose faces frowned up at me as I shuffled to the front door, knocking hurriedly, waiting.

Her grandmother offers me tea, manzanilla to calm nerves. She studies me without suspicion, reclining on a stuffed blue brocade chair, crocheting a multicolored wool blanket from scraps of thread — yellow, white, brown, black, red, turquoise — the colors blend into five-pointed star bursts linking patches of colored wool. Needles and thread are stored inside a black, pot-bellied fire-place in the middle of the home's central room. The rectangular room is furnished with a dark mahogany, four poster bed and an antique dining table. Three chairs with strips of paint shedding crusts of blue-green colors are pushed under the table. She places a hot tea mug on top of the fireplace which serves as both storage bin and coffee table in summer. Ermila's grandmother speaks candidly in a low, melodic woman's voice, *siéntate*.

The sturdy, spirited child crossed the *rio Bravo* when she was ten. She would outlive war, fights, and battles; she would witness lynchings during *la Revolución*. In San Luis Potosí, her family's small village of Piotillo, loyalties became difficult. Who to trust, the *maderistas*, the *carrancistas*, all wanted their land and crops. Her father had over- heard about Villa in the north and how people regarded him, but he was too far away to help. One day, her father was taken to the town square to be shot by a firing squad for not speaking to federal soldiers. He chose to stay home with his family and his children, to protect them, he said. But there were no choices, only battle and the promise of ro- mance in battlefields for young *soldados* and *soldaderas*. Her grandmother's tía, her fa- ther's younger sister, told the children to go to the town square to beg for mercy to save their father, to plead that he not be murdered the next morning. Ermila's *guilt* did what she had to do, screaming loudly, begging the exe- cutioners. By afternoon, her father towered over the doorway facing a grateful family, rays of light peaking from behind a giant figure. Within a month, the family gathered a few items, clothes, and a *molcahete*, enough to carry for the trip north. Ermila's *güelita* in- sisted sometimes one had to shout, to thun- der cries for all to hear because if a woman didn't roar at injustice, a day would come when all would be taken from her.

Her grandmother gave Ermila quiet encouragement to fight a town's conscience, one that wanted her censored. The town stifled loud, irreverent women, women expected to stay in their place, to spoil men, to listen to their troubles, and if wives or sisters disputed husbands or brothers, they were called *putas* or *jotas*. A woman's strength was judged by how she accepted her husband, no matter what kind of life he dealt her, drunkenness, womanizing, a slap or a firm word. This was the bargain of marriage.

Will this story end differently? Will Ermila win back peaceful dreams? Will she witness justice? There can be no happy ending, only in fantasy, what the mind chooses to make up, to hold on to as real. The imagination will dodge cruelty, escaping the crime — how the body has been pillaged, scarred — pretending this never happened, fooling memory with another meaning. She would live her life pretending, lying. If Ermila didn't bargain with it now, the act itself, the rape, the violation, would haunt her waiting to happen again in a memory that is so real that when the man behind a checkout stand glares at your breasts, you bear the shame all over again.

And men did ogle her, a vengeful scrutiny to tame her, nasty cat calls to frighten her. Men responded callously, listening to Pelón's defense of five men who raped her, all reasoning that theirs was not the crime.

"On Saturday nights, the men get excited," they said to reporters from the nearby city. "The guys had a little fun. Nobody got hurt. Not really, and anyway, she asked for it. She was always with somebody, in the back seat of a car, in alleys, she fucked anybody. Those men just gave her what she wanted."

These words were printed, convincing further those who were certain that a woman like Ermila needed punishment. Newspaper headlines announced her insatiable appetite for sex, reporting how the attorney had exposed her promiscuity with other men. When Pelón argued in court, where did he get his ideas? Were they testimony to his failing marriage? In college, he had accused the young woman of liking sex too much. Late at night, in my room, she would tell me how he insulted her.

In court, I study Ermila. She resurrects a puzzle daily. Surveying the courtroom, before me, appears the angelic face of the boy who had harmed me. Pelón calls the rapist a victim. The woman is absent, a consequence. Her injury is nothing to these men who decide she is their whore.

Ermila, *la malinchista*, *la chingada*, a betrayer, her own people called her. Her life began like savagery fighting to survive in her mother's womb. After two sons, her mother would attempt to abort Ermila. Unprepared to feed another child, the thirty-year-old mother jumped from the top floor of a church's staircase, tumbling to the bottom only to discover she still carried a baby. Later, she drank swigs of Pine Sol, swallowing so much she vomited all night. After six months of carrying the child, the mother sprung from where she stood on a kitchen chair, but the unborn baby stubbornly lived and a month later Ermila was born prematurely, staying in the hospital for weeks, causing an unnecessary expense, her mother complained. The daughter's life began fighting for survival.

At home, Ermila gave her brothers orders, at school, she defied her teachers, on the playground, she winced at Anglos, especially girls who wore crisp white blouses with loosely pleated cotton skirts. Ermila wanted to fly from this town, hungry for a life beyond muddy, pot-holed, gravel roads, eager to eat French food in restaurants with table clothes and fresh flowers. The smell of *fideo con carne* spiced with a garlic and coriander mixture, a smell she would crave years later, sickened her. Ermila, *la güedita* with auburn hair, honey skin, and yellow golden eyes, had plans to leave.

Her woman's body flourished at fifteen with full hips carrying muscular, shapely legs, rayon skirts blowing through them. She wore her brother's thin sleeveless T-shirts, braless, and swept her reddish-brown hair from her face with a thick red bandanna around her forehead marking a toughness. Dressed alluringly, she'd hang laundry in the back yard or saunter into town to buy groceries, swinging her hips. When her mother became too tired, frustrated and weak-willed, the middle-aged woman died giving birth to Ermila's baby sister. The young daughter diapered, fed, rocked, and slept in the same bed with the newborn; then cooked, mopped, and washed, for her brothers and father while a younger brother, who adored her, learned to iron shirts and khaki pants.

Evenings, Ermila opened her books attempting homework. After the dinner dishes, with a baby sister, now four years old, squatting near her at the kitchen table, she hovered over algebra problems. Her oldest brother, Pepito, had been an expert mathematician. His senior year, he had made A's in trigonometry and advanced calculus. When he was twelve, he had played with a used chemistry set he had found in a trash can in the Anglo neighborhood. Pepito, driven by math and science, would have graduated high school with honors and a scholarship to junior college, but something happened that year. He started coming home late, drugged, and disinterested when he crashed his shiny, nineteen fifty-four, two-tone Chevy sedan. A mechanically perfect, white and peach-colored car was parked in the middle of the front yard with the back end smashed, the passenger side doors were wrinkled metal. Something had disillusioned her oldest brother. Ermila wanted to ask him for help with her math homework, hoping he would gain interest in what had once excited him, but her brother just lay in an unlit bedroom listening to deadening music on his head-phones. She couldn't understand how or why he'd given up. Neighbors rumored about a white girl whose father shut the door on Pepito. He had tried to pick her up in a car he'd bought working double shifts bagging groceries at the HEB. But the car, like a rusted trophy, meant nothing anymore. Shortly before, the white girl had peeked from behind a curtain in her bedroom window as he climbed in the front seat and drove away.

Carolina's eyelashes stopped fluttering; Ermila closed a fat algebra book, silently. The baby had fallen asleep, her head still on the kitchen table, arms in her lap, tiny fingers twitching. Carrying the four year old to their bedroom and lying her on the bed, Ermila contemplated Carolina's innocent, peaceful face, a face which calmed her older sister as she brushed the baby's black curls.

At sixteen, Ermila's face also wore innocence, but hers was mingled with pain's wisdom. Already, she had experienced too much. When she spoke, she spoke directly, with purpose. With an arrogant air, she exhibited strength and sensuality. Men prized her provocative arrogance each assuming he would be the one to tame her. She provoked them to her side as she stepped on the sidewalk that led to town. Teen-aged boys observed older men who approached her; bantering, they placed an arm around her waist, but within a block, she'd throw off the man's arm, disappearing into an air-conditioned grocery store. Women weren't supposed to be that sure of themselves, that lustful and proud. Where did she learn these ways, this toughness?

Ermila played with peoples' weaknesses, listening to simple conversation, noting inane behavior. She observed them, then performed for the room filled with unsuspecting victims, dropping bombs about her childhood.

"When I was five, my father was drunk like always and he pushed me outside of the house and locked all the doors. It was raining. Thunder always scared me so he threw me outside yelling, "*Andalé chiquita, así se te quita lo medioso.*"

"I banged on the door, crying for an hour, maybe more, but he wouldn't let me in, so I stood in the middle of the back yard with my face up to the sky like a turkey who'll drown 'cause its too stupid to put its head down and close its beak. Rain got me all wet, but I didn't drown. I took off all my clothes and stood there naked waiting for lightning to hit me, but it didn't. After that I wasn't afraid of thunder anymore."

Articulating slowly, she witnessed each word land on people's faces. Savage little memories tailored a stubborn woman. Scarred, she'd expose herself, but only halves of herself. Never the whole truth because people never heard the whole story, never understood the fullness of one's experience, only half-stories, half-explanations were all she offered, leaving their imaginations to fill in who they wanted her to be, not who she was. She had become their rumor.

Ermila was no mystery. She was artless and naive to the town's people. Everyone empathized with her life story: the drunken father who couldn't hold a job; the mother who beat her two younger sons in frustration and cherished her oldest son, her favorite, ideal beauty. Her mother neglected an only daughter. When her mother died during childbirth, a baby girl became her sister's child, and although the young daughter was twelve and unprepared for motherhood, she became like the mother she had always wanted.

Childhood scars were temporal wounds, invisible reminders, but for her, as visible as branded flesh, like a burn from cooking, the direct contact with fire stings swiftly, but the scar from the burn is marked on skin, a reminder of things forgotten. These were Ermila's scars, recognized by outsiders with keen insight to spy through wounded behavior. Few could see them, but they were there. Her own skin had grown too thick to feel what strangers guessed.

The sixteen year old appealed to senses. Smell, scent, sight, textures, she could temper shrewdly. No one was surprised when the *bolillo*, whose father owned the furniture store, fell in love with Ermila. Standing at a window, behind a bedroom chest, he sneaked looks as she passed by the store, roaming into town to pay the light bill at the HEB. She deliberately traced the route past the store's window, alluringly self-aware. By the time she reached the end of the block, she had hooked him. His virgin ways spotted her lustiness. None of the white girls in high school flounced like that, breasts proudly bobbing in air. White girls wore proper, button down collars to hide their sex, but the golden-skinned poor girl carried secrets between her broad, lovely thighs, recognizing what boys begged to learn. Her older brothers didn't like the rich *bolillo* Ermila allowed into their house. He was a blond, football player who drove a bright red, Ford Mustang and called them spics, sneering jokingly. Ermila's brothers believed *el bolillo* used their little sister the way white boys used the girls in their *pueblito*, branding them easy girls with reputations. Her younger brother observed the *bolillo* jealously.

To escape El Pueblo, Ermila would trade herself to a white boy hoping he'd leave and take her with him. She ignored racist words that inferred he couldn't appreciate her world. But after she heard him, repeatedly, make the same stupid remarks about "greasers" or announce loudly, "the wetbacks are back," pointing at her brothers who entered their own house, she'd berate him calling him an idiot gringo *pendejo* who didn't know anything about anybody. She had no patience or tolerance for his ignorance, incapable of easing him into awareness; she was born impatient and intolerant.

"Don't let 'em treat you like that, papá," she scorned her father's bosses. At the Chevy dealer, where he worked as janitor, the gringos gave him orders daily.

"Manny, bring me coffee," "Manny, mop this floor," "Manny, come here and move these shelves, fill the paper towels, don't forget to wipe the sinks, scrub the toilets." "Haven't you finished yet, you 'ol wetback?"

Her father would grin at his superiors, "Meester Smeet, Meester Langly, I wanna you to mit my *hija*, Ermila."

Politely, they'd say hello, but as soon as her father turned his back, they'd gape at her breasts through her sleeveless, white T-shirt, asking her out for a drink even though she was only sixteen.

Distrust was her weapon. She couldn't explain, she argued; soft explanations didn't become her. People found her impatient, angry, hard, but some saw her beauty, rare like rose gold. In the courtroom, I spotted her, admiring her resilience. After the court session one day, I met her, morbidly questioning her like so many others. Diffidently, she talked to me, repeating what she had said to the police, over and over, to lawyers and psychologists, over and over, the same report. I'd heard parts of the story in the courtroom, read it in newspapers, but I wanted more from her. I wanted to hear through her quiet rage. I recognized her composure, her absolute control.

They claimed they didn't hurt her. The five men in the car that night said they hadn't meant to harm her. "Just have some fun, fuck her, slap her once or twice. Some women liked a little roughness," they announced.

Chencho, the loud one, saw her strutting on the side of the road. He screamed to her. Obscenities. Casually, she yelled, "*Pinche puto*," and continued a slow pace, ignoring him. Her response enraged him, but outrage also fed his sexual hunger.

At thirty-five, Chencho boasted his behavior in front of younger men; he gained approval from older brothers who taught him how to be, how to survive in a small town that gossiped about their mother and a non-existent father. Everyone gossiped about the Anglo trucker who would come to town twice a year to stay with *la costurera*. The red-haired, freckled-skinned man parked his rig in the front yard and slept in the bedroom with *la costurera*. She'd send the young boys to their grandmother's house to spend the night when the red-haired Anglo came to town. But as they grew older, *la costurera* assumed her sons would become accustomed to the gringo. They never did. They hated him.

The *costurera's* son was skinny, short, not muscular or sturdy like the other rapists, but petite with soft white hands and milky skin. Black curls framed his fleshy baby's cheeks. His *abuelita* named him Inocencio after her younger brother who had died at four months in an accident no one discussed. *La abuelita* saw her baby brother drown when they crossed *el rio Bravo* looking for their father. Her mother crossed following a man who traveled north for a job with the railroad, aware that he was eluding her and his children for a woman who lived in some border town on the gringo side. The wife never found him. Her own daughter suspected a mother wanted to punish a father or save a baby boy from misery, but the careless accident hadn't seemed like carelessness.

His *abuelita*, a plump woman with jet black dyed hair, spoiled Inocencio. On days when she would hang the laundry to dry in the backyard, she settled him on the bed in the bedroom facing the yard. He would pore eyes over her, then cry out, just to see her move swiftly on short chubby legs wrapped in nylons coiled below the knees to hold them up. His grandmother ran to the open window obeying the young boy's requests. She'd bring him a *galletita* from the kitchen, kiss his forehead, then go back to work. Pleased, the baby boy, Chenchito, munched on his vanilla wafer.

An older brother showed Chenchito things about sex, things not for a little boy, not yet. As he grew older, an uncle, his mother's brother, would frequent their house. The nephews liked him, played with him, but the youngest one, the one who was so pretty, the uncle liked him best. Twenty years between them did not keep the uncle and nephew from being inseparable. When the boy became a teenager, they went to baseball games, to cock fights, things he would have done with a father. But the uncle became too familiar. He raped the boy, kept raping him until the boy was strong enough to beat up the old man and spit in his face.

More and more, when he drove to the city, he snuck into men's bars, fooling himself, convincing himself he was there to spy on men from El Pueblo, "to check on queers," he'd lie. Men would straddle a bar stool beside him. The regular customers saw him every few weeks. They recognized his type, confused yet eager to prove he wasn't weak or soft. Most of the men avoided him. They sensed Chencho was trouble, but sometimes one of them would slide next to him, grazing Chencho's elbow, a preemptive sign. Gruffly, under his breath, Chencho mumbled, not wanting to be understood.

Once drunk, he'd slip outside to the parking lot. A stocky man with thin hair combed forward to cover a bald spot would drive up. He'd jump in the car, go to a stranger's apartment, have sex, and pass out from alcohol, smelling like poppers. In the dark, he'd open his eyelids and pillage through the man's wallet robbing five twenty-dollar bills. Slamming the door behind him, Chencho rushed into stultifying air. The man who resembled his uncle didn't stop *la costurera's* son from stealing. The old, bald man with a paunchy stomach blinked at a wall next to his bed when the door slammed.

During the trial, he would go to bars. One night, someone Chencho had never seen ordered a beer, and asked him plainly, without hesitation, why he'd done that to Ermila. Chencho mumbled into his glass. Dazed, searching white foam, he said she'd asked for it.

"Everybody makes bets on whose gonna fuck that *puta* next."

The man who faced Chencho was husky,

athletic, and under an unbuttoned shirt were pumped arm muscles. On his stomach were scars, lines shaping a design. Shrapnel had done this. A friend had told him the loud rapist had been here. He grabbed the loud rapist by the collar, whispering once, quickly and clearly.

"You come in here again, my friends and me, we'll take you in the back room and we'll shove a broomstick where you want it. We'll do that and more, next time you come in here."

He released Chencho's collar throwing the skinny frame back on the stool. The *costurera's* son jumped up, red-faced, storming outside into damp stillness. Beside his truck, he bent over and threw up. Bristling, frantic, he wanted to go back, he needed to go back, to rest, to think. The bar was the only place he sustained any peace these days. They'd left him alone before. He heard them snicker when they saw him stride in, but they'd leave him alone. Now, he had nowhere. In the courtroom the town's people either pitied or scorned him. And Pelón, Pelón painted Chencho the victim, frail and vulnerable.

Pelón defended the thirty-five year old rapist. Sympathetically, he spoke, "We all suffer, we're all victims." The rapist looked grim for the jurors as Pelón cross-examined a court-appointed psychologist, asking about a rapist's temper. The psychologist described rapists, repeat offenders, repeating what they had learned as children.

Ermila's attorney sketched a scene of a lake with a sun, setting or rising. In the middle of the water, a man's figure, gripping a fishing rod, hunched over in a boat. Protruding from his back was a knife. Beads of sweat ran down the prosecutor's pasty, chubby face. Nauseated by the courtroom's muggy stench, he claimed the Mexicans who filled the room daily smelled like a filthy urinal. Planning a fishing trip with his son, the pasty man hoped the trial would end soon. His wife would not forgive him if he canceled the vacation to defend a Mexican girl who said she had been raped by a few greasers.

Mexican girls cleaned their house and most of them were honest, hard-working, but every now and then, his wife would find cans of Spam missing or stored clothes would begin to disappear. The gray-haired Anglo woman would fire the ones who stole. "Even when they're born in this country, Mexican girls just aren't raised to be decent," she'd complain, her voice squeaky. Glancing up from his newspaper at the woman who mopped the kitchen, his eyes landed on nipples visible through the white cleaning uniform his wife obliged them to buy and wear. Sweat had trickled from her neck to her breasts, suspended on wet nipples. He grunted in agreement as he riveted his eyes back to his morning paper.

The men who judged Ermila excused the boys, "they're just mischievous, that's all." "But what about Ermila?" I asked myself. "What about Ermila?" I repeat silently.

The young woman from El Pueblo is seated a row behind Pelón. At the opposite end of the courtroom, behind Ermila, I lean forward to catch a glimpse of the young woman's face. Surreptitiously, she turns her head sideways, without looking back, the corner of her eye meets mine. I'm wondering what she speculates about Pelón's defense, remembering nights when she came to my door with bruises he stamped on her flesh, coming to me, to yell, to shriek, to blame. His blows were my fault, she accused. During the trial she would phone me. She missed me. Why wouldn't I see her, to talk, to be friends, we'd been friends before. Why was I so distant, so distrusting? What had she done except try to love me, she pleaded. But in the courtroom, she is shy, secretive, afraid Pelón would catch her eye's scan in my direction.

❑

I bit her tongue. Maliciously, I bit again,
harder. Her hand, stroking my hair, clenched
a fist, and yanked hard. My head jerked back,
blood trickled from her wound to my bottom
lip. She wiped the blood with her thumb, confused, injured, but not angry. Desperate, she
followed me, maybe afraid I'd leave again.
And yet when I would finally agree to meet
her, she could barely look at me. And I, I only
grew angrier and more fierce with each pas-
sive look she cast.

Unexpectedly, unannounced, she arrived at
my brother's house where I slept in a back
bedroom during the trial. My brother answered her knock at the door. From the bedroom, I heard their laughter. Men, charmed
by her, savored her charm, her ceremonious
beauty. My brother came to my bedroom,
knocked on the door and whispered, "Guess
who's here?" When I opened the door he
raised his eyebrows and held up his truck
keys to signal he was leaving. Without another word, he stepped quietly down the hallway, opened the kitchen door and drove away.

Jealousy overcame me. A vindictive, hateful
jealousy. I wanted to possess her. To insist she

was mine. I lied to myself, bragging that I wouldn't let her use me anymore.

In the living room, her back is turned. She studies family photographs on the wall, caught by a three by five photo of my brother and me, we are four and six years old, both dressed in mallow pink. I'm wearing a pink dress with white ruffles on the hem and black patent leather shoes that shine. My light brown hair is gathered in a pony tail stretching my face's skin. He wears brown, pleated, cotton pants, a pink blazer, and brown cowboy boots with pink stitching on the sleeves. We're not smiling. We gape into the camera with wide, frightened eyes as if shocked by a crackling bulb's light. When she turns to face me, she's smiling from the picture of my childhood.

I'm angry she's here. My face frightens her; she subdues fear and embraces me. Her suppleness excites and repels. At first, I'm silent. She addresses me with meaningless chatter, kissing my mouth. A savage kiss. I bite her tongue. Draw blood. She's hurt. I am my only real witness.

In a corner of a room, a woman shrieks, screeching louder, pounding on a back with clenched fists. A precise rage. Moving closer to slap, to choke, kicking a living room chair, grabbing photographs two at a time from a wall, smashing them. Glass flies. A piece lodges on a left forearm. A photo of childhood lies shattered. Crouching, arms folded over her head, a terrified child huddles in a corner. A swift figure flees through the front door, crushing glass and photos. Red blood drips round spots on the sidewalk, leaving a trail.

She comes after me. I jog faster. I can't look at her, I won't look. There are no tears in my eyes. The young woman catches me, clutches an injured arm and tugs me back to my brother's house. Words are not spoken. She leads me into the bathroom where she finds tweezers, iodine, and gauze to treat the injury. As she pulls the thin, sharp glass from my arm's soft underside, my tears flow as easily as the blood spurting from my flesh. The young woman licks my arm, swirling lips round and round, smearing her cheeks, then my mouth, up and down; chin, lips, forehead are dabbed and anointed. She is pleased with her victory, a crimson victory, self-satisfied to eye longing on my face.

Throughout the trial, I hated her. She, with her husband and his rapists, so proud, refusing to reclaim Ermila. I was like Ermila, not in strength or courage, but in her appetite for vengeance.

❏

One morning, driving to court, I fill my car with gas. I saw him, his chocolate face and hands, his arms taut. He pumped gas, offering no sign that he recognized me. With my charge card in his hand, he blinked at the sight of my name.

"It's you," Juan said.

"Yes, it's me."

"You're here for the trial." He didn't ask, but instead stated what he thought was true.

His easy manner amused me, not at all curious about the last ten years, but neither was I. He stuffed my card in his shirt pocket, wiped the front windshield, then placed a stained rag in a back pant pocket. Searching my eyes, he leaned on the car's door frame with his elbow on the roof. A refined chest and narrow waist were accentuated with each movement. Our last night on the beach as our bodies swayed with the warm waves, we had confessed faults and abuses.

"Those guys, especially that loud scrawny one needs a lesson for doing what he did."

When I attend the trial, I dream of *la costurera's* son. He leaps, carrying lean forelegs down a paved highway. A full moon casts his shadow as he darts by, like twins racing. Out of the shadows, a short-haired dog sprints, chasing the *costurera's* son. The white dog pounces. They fall to the ground. The animal hovers over him, sniffing, then strides away proudly, head up, nose toward the sky. The *costurera's* son bolted up and wept, his left leg ripped, bleeding from the white dog's teeth.

The loud rapist is born at childhood. The boy-child frequented men's bars to assuage his pain, but he couldn't quell the memories. He tried hard to suppress boyhood memories, the days when his uncle would find him playing in a vacant house next door. It was here where things he could not forget happened. It was here where he began to grip confusion, thrilled by the man he hated, the one who covered the length of his back and legs. The boy, thrown to the ground would lie on his stomach, a right arm wrapped around his throat, choking him; a left hand covered his mouth, a body invaded his.

In school yards he and other boys chased girls. They would chase a girl, letting her scramble to prolong the game. She would scream, an exhilarating scream, the kind girls holler on roller coaster rides. When they caught her, she would fall rolling on the ground. Three or four of the boys would sur-round her, one of them, usually the *cos-*

turera's son, would pull down her underwear. She would squirm and squeal. The boys, scoffing, would march away heroically.

At drive-in theaters, his games with girls got rougher, with his same schoolyard friends, the same three or four boys with one girl. They'd tease her and prep her with Southern Comfort, a smooth, sweet whisky. In the back seat Chencho slowly began to finger her nipples through cloth. Rubbing softly, he offered her a full glass, unbuttoned her blouse and played the usual game. They'd ask her to guess who sucked her nipples. She'd scream, *"Así, así"* tittering from ticklish tongues. She wanted him; she didn't behave otherwise. He'd only invite girls popular for their reputation. They couldn't resist his handsome white face, his thin nose, and the black curls that fell on his forehead. He wore tight blue jeans and a black leather motorcycle jacket, looking timid and worn. Wealthy girls giggled when he swaggered his hips in hallways, sensing he was too dangerous for them, but wanting him anyway. He pursued girls with bee-hive hair, snugly-fit skirts, and low-cut sweaters. Offering shots of sweet whiskey, he waited until the chosen girl for the night became relaxed and silly. After pushing the other boys from the back seat, Chencho prepared himself. In one smooth move he pulled her skirt up and underwear down; unbuttoning his jeans with a quick jerk he shoved himself inside. As he licked her breasts, she moaned quietly. He kept at it. Pumping her. The boys in the front seat hurried him, wanting their turn. Ignoring them, Chencho lifted her legs, wrapping them around his waist tightly.

In a dream, he finds me. He chases, attacks. His hands grappling breasts, arms, legs, mouth, suffocating me. I can't wake up. I try to scream, to shout her name, my young woman's name. The sound of my voice shakes me.

I'll forget my past. I'll forget the young girl who committed acts of vengeance by selling herself to worn-out ugly men to pay other worn-out ugly men who make laws. I didn't want to tell you this about me. You judge me. But this too was my life, a life beyond a memory of the young woman from El Pueblo. But you suspected that. There were other times, times I don't speak about. I hated myself then, hated how I turned myself over, a young body traded like spoils to hustlers, swindlers. In and out of rooms where men sat fat or lean behind desks smoking cigars. They move you to the couch in their office, squat down, unzip their pants and shove your head. You gag. Your eyes look up, checking the door or a window, a passage to flee. You become ugly. For money. You live an uneasy fear, never sure who the man is, what he'll want, the way he'll want it. You're not like women who service men casually, in and out of rooms, frivolously.

Those days plague me, my stomach nauseous. It comes back, that mood, when I was a young girl. No one will want me, love me, care about me. No one will say I'm worthy of anything. Of love, for example. Those words are nowhere near me.

Why the memory? Maybe to be fair about how I represent her. I, too, am not so guiltless, so pure. Dreams cease with age, disillusion unfolds. People lie. Calling us perverse, abnormal, privileged even. They would say things, hurtful things. Joy could no longer be found in our bedrooms and kitchens.

This Los Angeles was for me, like her store owner's stinking cot.

I awaken, cloaked by death; its shield protects me. I'm trapped between visions and that which I intuit, never sure what's real, but always conscious of how I'm scorned, hated, rejected for who and what I am. Mexican, dumb, stupid, hateful, ugly, someone who must learn a world that craves tanned brown, not real brown, not birth brown, just gringo-tanned-at-the-beach, golden brown, not Mexican brown. Dark-honey-brown, a grade school teacher called me once. "You are a dark-honey-brown, I envy your color," she said for all the *gringuitos*, but I discerned the mockery.

One day I released a powerfully strong pocket of gas from a stomach that churned from nervousness. I crouched in a desk, alone, while white kids spoke a different language. I let out gaseous air, an odor overpowered their smell. They gawked at me, "It's the Mexican who eats beans," they confided to each other. Uneasiness and worry caused me to rebel.

The trial dragged on, surreal, protracted. Days were severed by nights and weekends away from the courthouse. The events clouded a quiet town.

People acted strangely. No one could be trusted. They eyed each other in public places wondering whose side each defended. Most of the men agreed with Pelón that the Anglo media pictured them like greasy boys with slicked back hair, baggy chino slacks and plaid untucked shirts. Women may have objected, but most were cowards, afraid to lose husbands or lovers. The same women who would not condemn the rapists, accused Ermila, that she complained too much, that she dressed too provocatively. These were Ermila's enemies; wives who feared reproach from husbands, wives who would stress, "Yes, men aren't fair, but they can't change, that's how they are." "Ermila shouldn't dress in tight low-cut blouses or in her brother's T-shirts with no bra." She didn't deserve to be raped, they argued, but she shouldn't behave so aggressively, fighting publicly, calling men names, aggravating them. Maybe she'd think twice the next time she embarrassed a man in front of his friends by telling him his *verga* was "*una tripa seca.*"

At home, Pelón checked his wife's face, her attitude, her movements. She had conceded, believing his reasons for defending the young men, but since I'd returned, his wife judged him, yet carefully hid her disapproval. Once, when he came home early, she cried on the bedroom telephone; she pleaded, shouted, then whimpered. He lounged in the front room reading the newspaper. Muffled words crept through thin walls and when she entered, surprised to see him, a guilty look crossed her face. Disguising her guilt, his wife embraced him, "It's good to see you home early." He didn't ask about the phone call; she didn't tell him, instead probing about the trial. Frustrated, he answered, "Too many outsiders who don't get it about this town anymore keep interfering."

His wife listened quietly, but refrained from

discussing the trial with him further. If she reacted, they would fight. After so many years, she learned to feign disinterest. He tested her, tested how she'd react. Pelón scorned her silence, reading her restraint as resistance, even though she was convinced he read compliance on her face. But he guessed what the silence and the phone call meant, that she would be with me soon. And he would fight with his wife again.

Pelón had visions that night. In terror, he awoke, cold from sweat, grabbing a floppy penis, frightened by the same grisly nightmare since the trial began. In the darkness, he argues with me. I scream at him, "You believe those *desgraciados!*"

"They're young boys, they just need help, some guidance."

"Yeah, sure, young *pendejos* who treat women like a bunch of *putas.*"

"What do you want from me. *Mira ten esto. Pontelo tú!*" He holds a sharp six inch blade in his right hand, the wooden handle indented. He clutches the shining knife. In a swift gesture he slashes his penis, holding it in his left hand. I refuse it, gazing blankly at him as he grips a bleeding, puny genital. Pelón awoke with a moan, shaking. The bed sheets were soaked throughout. Urgently, he looked for his wife. She slept peacefully.

He couldn't admit to her how I haunted his

nights. He wouldn't discuss his panic until he was sure enough time had passed hoping she'd forgotten to tell me about his fears. On these nights, he couldn't trust her, preferring to fall into troubled sleep, but of course, he was right not to trust her. Years later, she would confess everything to me in letters and phone calls.

Fantasies of me would awaken her to cool, damp sheets. As he slept, she would glide her hand across his clammy back. Since the trial, she would wake to his tossing and try to comfort his apprehension. He had bad dreams, but he wouldn't admit them, and she wouldn't ask, perhaps wanting him to suffer. When she couldn't fall asleep again, the young woman found herself facing the ceiling, fantasizing about me. She reflected on times in high school when we shared bedrooms with twin beds. In junior college, she would come to my dorm room, often drunk, sometimes pleading, not sure why she pleaded. The young woman wanted me, but couldn't say, waiting for the words, "*No te vayas*," to be uttered from my mouth.

A spring night, she was with Pelón. They drank tequila, she downed a shot with salt and lemon, but no more than one. Consciously, she planned. He drove her back to her room at midnight where they fumbled quick sex, then he left, driving back to the city, lying that he would study. Sober, she bolted across campus, gripping the glass bottle's neck, and knocked on my door. Behind the door, I call her name, only she would come this late. I open the door groggy from sleep, trying to pull her into the dark room. Hesitant, she stands in a hallway lit by a single bald bulb, asking if I'm alone.

We drink shots of tequila from the mouth of the bottle, making a fist, licking the thumb and forefinger, pouring salt, licking again and swigging the bottle, then sucking a slice of lemon. We make faces, comically. We finish the bottle. The young woman from El Pueblo becomes irritable, unquiet. We argue. About nothing and everything. About Pelón. I threaten to leave her. I would go to Los Angeles. I wouldn't stay while she was his. But tonight, after malicious words mar each of us, the young woman cried. I held her, kissed her tears, licked her face, found her mouth.

Her husband tossed in bed, she searched the bedroom's shadows, finding the moonlight, striving for memories of that night. She remembers how she woke at dawn on a single twin bed, in my arms. She remembers velvety arms. We kiss frantically; tongue and fingers induce her cries. Every night, she will run to me. We become contorted bodies and emotions. I beg the young woman to escape with me, but she falters. Between kisses and tears, she promises she'll come, knowing she'd stay with him in El Pueblo. He'd go away to law school, she'd marry him, go with him, they'd return to El Pueblo. This was his plan. After unspeakable nights together, the young woman censored her passion, gave in, chose a common, predictable life.

Lying in his bed, staring at his sticky back, realizing mistakes were only mistakes, she resented that I would not forgive her. During the trial the young woman phoned me at my brother's house. My brother often lied for me, announcing I wasn't in, but she'd heard me in the background, "Tell her I'm not here." That day, I answered the phone. The young woman's voice asked me to join her. She needed to explain why she went to the trial, why she sat behind Pelón. I listened. Relentless, she pleaded, begged, screamed, then begged again. Finally, I say, yes, I'll see you, but not in his house. Somewhere else, but not there. She knew I'd come anyway.

I don't submit easily. But sometimes I meet someone who pries me open with ease. And then I give. Am I admitting she was someone who could do that? No, I'm reminding myself I'd met women who could. I didn't need her anymore, not since high school when I believed she was the only one I'd ever want beside me.

Her phone calls. She tried to reminisce, to re-create awkward nights on a twin bed in my dorm room. I buried those nights, forgot them, but the day in her kitchen reminded me. I stood at her doorway, his doorway. I promised myself I would not go back and each time I broke down, unable to resist her. Nervous, I wondered when he'd interfere.

She wears black. It's early summer. Orange-crimson azaleas bloom and she wears a black tailored blouse tucked inside a black skirt. My hands will pause at her waist, then slide down her hips. Focusing eyes on mine, she presses breasts against me. Warm. The gesture distracts. She grins, turning to face the kitchen sink, washing strawberries. I pick a plump one, placing ripe flesh in her mouth. She closes her eyes to dwell on me.

I imagine, in the tight black cotton, her pores can barely breathe. My eyes land on her hips. She teases, tempting purposefully, looking away. The chase, I thought, she recreates the chase and I'll follow. She is so sure I'll follow, into the bedroom, into some private corner where I can't resist. In the corner against a hallway wall, I thrust myself against her, brushing my hand steadily up her leg, under her skirt. Tightening my grip on her ass, she raises her leg, placing her foot on a table next to the wall, giving my hand access. I want her more. My fantasies race ahead. She rubs against me. I shove harder against the wall. I unbutton my blue shirt. She sucks nipples cautiously, guarding herself. Her body hesitates, but mine does not. Fast sex binds us. Her hands hug my neck pushing my face into the crevice between her neck and shoulder. I rest safely. Satisfied. I thrive on these moments when she pulls me close. I want her to pull me close, closer, infinitely.

A car door slams; we hurry back to the kitchen.

But he isn't home, not yet. He would be soon. Slowly, I drink my coffee, tell her I want her, I want to undress her, suck her nipples, I want her body on mine so I can coast my hands down her back to caress her ass. She wasn't embarrassed when I spoke boldly. She enjoyed the words. We had this, a language of desire to frustrate, to satisfy. Language arouses her. I greet pleading in her eyes.

Here's the scenario, I say to you. I've come back, but not to find you.

You don't believe me, you say I'm here for you and I suppose you're right.

But I'll deny it at first. Instead, I tell you a story. Your story. I tell you how you've left him. You live on an island now, your island of deep sea blue with green plants, orange and violet flowers. You're with someone else. A man, a somewhat passionless, yet reliable man. You have children. Two beautiful, playful children, like you. You live for these children of yours. I have come to you, to greet you again. I'm not afraid to be honest with you, maybe because you're so far away. I come to your house on this island where people are deliciously dark skinned and dark-eyed, by the hundreds zigzagging on city streets on humid nights, brushing against each others' damp torsos. Bright colors are constant. I meet him, this man you've chosen as the father of your children. He is unsuspecting, kind. We drink espressos. I get up to leave, kiss your mouth, shake his hand, hug your children. We pretend the visit is over. We will not receive each other again.

The next day, your naked body fulfills me. We lie on the floor, on a blanket, in a deserted house on the beach far from the city where you live. You asked me to meet you here. I surprised you when I found it. The detective in me can never resist searching for you, finding you again and again. We make love with the usual hunger, the usual craving. We satisfy each other only to begin again after a few moments pass. I ask, do you come here with other lovers. I sense the father of your children is too common to satisfy your appetite for the bizarre.

You answer, yes, you come here with

women and men, but not as often as I think, and romantically you turn to me to say, in each of them you look for me. I laugh, and so do you. You haven't stopped lying to me and I haven't stopped wanting your lies. Unlike our youth, we're sensible about romance, its idealism. You mock me and I don't care. I only want you this moment. The memory will delight me after today.

I leave you on your island, you're happy. I'm content to see you this way. This is the story. Your story.

"Do you think we can end like this?" I ask you.

You look at me, almost sad. You like the story, you tell me. You've always liked my stories, but they were never anything but that. You want to shake me back to reality. You want to talk about Pelón.

"He doesn't hit me anymore," you say.

"So you stay?" I ask.

"He's sorry for the bad years, but it was because of us."

"You blame us? Me? I made him hit you? So did he stop after I left?"

"He was more relaxed. He thought we'd finally be happy because you were gone."

"And now that I'm back?"

"Now that you're back, he's afraid again. He threatened me one night, but then he cried."

I don't feel the compassion you think you'll arouse in me. I never liked him, so its easy to ignore your plea.

"That's it? You believe he's changed? Does he know I'm here. Today?"

"No, it would hurt him," you whisper. "Please leave." You look down unable to greet my eyes. You've had me again. And again you're filled with guilt. Again, you insist it is only he you've betrayed.

My brother's phone rang that night. When I answered, steady, rhythmic breathing, Pelón's breathing, warned me, as if to tell me he wasn't a fool. He'd sighted my car parked in his driveway, but he drove on, waiting until I left before he entered his own home.

I became too honest. I don't mean with myself, I mean with strangers. I said too much, risking betrayal. I took risks in public, fighting with people I didn't like, barking orders and requests no one could meet. I became someone to hate. I hated myself.

Desire

¿Y qué buscabas en aquel sueño?

Migraciones
Gloria Gervitz

Her hold on me will not cease. After the trial, in Los Angeles, she controls me in yet another way, in unexplainable ways unknown to me, unfathomable to my conscious habits.

Daydreams were about her, but at night, I obliged myself to seek other women. I knelt before them, plunging my face between women's thighs in prayer. Again, I found women who soothed me, again, I fooled myself, believing I'd forget her in other women's beds.

She wouldn't let me go. I didn't want to go. I was trapped in common abuse. We screamed, demanded, had little or no peace. She became frantic when I screamed this at her, that our time together was coming to a close, a circle would close. We prepared for separate futures. We prepared for separation.

When the trial ended, I left, deceived by her, by Pelón, by El Pueblo. But she, the young woman, came with me. Every night, in dreams, she committed trespasses. Every night, we invented fresh lies.

I began new with old habits. I pretended as I
had when I was a child. I pretended nothing
changed after the acts against my body, I pretended I hadn't changed. I silenced the
screams for years, decades, the way I silence
desire for her. I lie to my body, to my psyche, I
lie to those around me. I mouth to myself that
meeting her, the way we met, that this too
has no meaning, will have no meaning. And
so I begin again with the young woman from
El Pueblo. I begin that which feels new, but is
not. And each time I have predicted my life
will shift, will finally reverse itself, but no, I
will begin to desire her and desire will fuel
more delusions. There will be whole days
when I won't remember why I live where I
live, there will be days when I won't want to
live. I will contemplate savage deaths, my
own and others. I will mastermind my death
to rid my body of her. I will dream of ways to
commit the act because desiring her is the
nightmare that won't end.

I plan my suicide. I don't tell her I'm planning my death. When I confess, she's not surprised. She expects it, not at all sorry I'm so
desperate that I could take a knife, like I did
when I was a child of four or five, that I would
take a knife and slash deeply into my stomach. She dissociates from my misery.

El Pueblo doesn't matter, not anymore. It's

now you who haunts me, who deludes me with language I've never heard before, language I've yearned for. You speak cleverly, you're so clever. Your tales of love are flirtatious. You stay. Long into the night. You fool me. I meet you at my door. We stand at its entrance, door open, not inside, not outside, only at its entrance. We stand. Exiled. People tiptoe by, peeking at us exiled in a doorway. When I start to close the door, I don't draw you in. You pause, then enter. That is how you dishonored me after so many years apart. I misread your kindness, mistook it for a wish.

Then you leave, you walk away on grassy knolls, jeans ripped at your waist, you conjure up someone else, you ponder him as you walk away.

A beggar, a drifter crouches before you for hours, for days, without moving, except to brush your cheek with her hand.

I could bluff and say that was all I needed or wanted from you, and so I did. And all the while, you ignored me, begging before you. I wanted you for the sake of wanting you and I wanted no one to take you from me. I held your memory. No one knew. I told no one.

Insanity infuses me. Do you see why I herald

you as my story unfolds? This is how you begin in my life again. Like this. And this is how I will relive the past in the present.

I came face to face with lunacy, with hallucinations. The normal, the common, that was unreal for me. So I questioned what others ordained to be normal as if their lives were something to entreat.

The young woman from El Pueblo offers herself, older and more tolerant, a mature aging face with laugh lines. She has a new talent, that of mapping the heart, where she transmits lovers' messages to each other, and to me.

Her hair sleek, dark, and peppered gray, falls around her cheeks, neck, shoulders, luxurious; her skin is brown like creamy coffee. She unveils sensuality, the way she reclines in a chair, legs crossed, one over the other, leaning into the frame, an arm up, cradled on the chair's back, her body offers dualities, closed yet open. A blouse hangs from her left shoulder exposing elegance. A premeditated gesture. She disrupts my sleep. I lie awake, eyelids fluttering, half-conscious.

Confessing, I plead for absolution. I utter secrets. *La costurera's* son. She listens, then tells me a story. Her childhood unravels. I envy her courage.

I don't know when I realized I was crazy, that I was as diseased as the world, the one I hated, criticized. But my hallucinations loomed as if real. Madness could have motive. What I planned came easily. The time had come. I mustered courage to help me execute the loud rapist, the *costurera's* son, to purge him from my nightmares, the ones that kept me tied to the woman from El Pueblo.

Was this premeditated murder? Had I planned his slaughter, had I calculated how to bludgeon his head with a fat, wooden, base-ball bat? Was a recurring nightmare premeditation?

She is lying on my bed. A dizziness like vertigo has overcome her. I ask her to explain exactly how she feels, lying on my bed. Faint, she says, and weak. Her head reels from words we spoke, inviting words, pleasing words: our weaknesses. I confess to her lyrically. She invokes the lyrical in me, the text spoken, or unspoken. Missed meanings land in air, quickly grasped by the one or the other. Sometimes we speak too many words to explain the obtuse, the not so obvious, the

Emma Pérez

undeclared.

With my fingertips, I reach for your mouth to
silence frustration. You let me touch you. Suddenly, I'm awake, I realize, you're the woman
I thirst for here in this desert called my heart.

Like a child, I beg you. I'm not above begging
you. You decide our lives are tangled and
tricky. You, a magician who delivers illusion,
you trick me with double images. You're here,
then you're gone.

You doubt me, how I want you. You want
me to prove my love, to renounce all others,
but you won't ask. You're not prepared for
someone like me. You send me away, order
me away. You can't love me, can't say it,
won't say it, the words jammed in your
throat. Stifled. Instead, you taunt me. I want
you to confess you love me. I want your
tongue to utter the sound my ears plead for.
My request amuses you. These are words re-
served for someone else, for him.

Every nerve ending erupts like fire. I panic.
I ache. For words you spoke once, *"No te
vayas."* Words to shrink my fears. You want to
forget me. You will. I panic more. My stomach
cramps. I would devour you if I could, possess
you, nourish you, but I can't. I don't know
how.

In the night, you're gone, then you reappear.

We're too serious, you advise. I wonder if we have a chance at love. You laugh at us, how our seriousness, our drama makes us foolish. I laugh with you. I feel so much pleasure in your laughter. The pleasure of your laughter falls on my face.

You're dangerous, she announces, repeating herself. I don't know what she means. She won't explain. Again, she alleges that I'm dangerous. Maybe she guessed what I had to do, that I wouldn't endure another loss, that I refused to mourn for her anymore.

Each day you forget me. Distance separates us. Hours, days, months pass. I don't believe in love anymore. I quit believing. In my head, your phrases etch promises. I see you in my mind's eye, animated, arms expressive, cutting through empty space as you report stories. You perform vividly. A romantic beauty. You read to me. Like a lover, you read. As if to prove you love me. I tingle from your voice's eroticism. I daydream. Your absence causes me to picture you. Your lips reach for mine. Your gaze, your touch, your voice lure me. Under the table, your leg presses against mine, carelessly. As if to go unnoticed. Do you know how your touch incites me, under the table.

You stand behind me. I linger in your chair, at your desk, reading your stories. You scribble in margins of manuscripts revising your method. I try to unravel you, your riddles. *Eres cuentista.* I wonder if I'll ever appear in your stories about trees and silences. I wonder if I've become so much a part of you that your landscapes of *el campo* will have as background someone you convinced you loved. Will you describe a woman who walked toward you one day, far in the distance, across a plaza, you see her roving, two women at her side, one hand in a jean pocket, boots noisily approach; her outline becomes full size. You smile a crooked, intuitive smile, a curve that curls your mouth's right corner. The smile draws her close. You are aware of the magic in your crooked smile. That moment, the woman who ambled across the plaza to greet you didn't know you would break her so completely.

Your nearness jars me. Behind me, you stand; I gasp quietly from thinning air. I can't breathe. I don't open my mouth to sound words. Any sound would reveal too much. You don't kiss my neck with your lips. You kiss me with warm breath. Your empathic breath lands on my neck, streams down to my breasts waiting for your tongue. Waiting still.

I remember how you teased. You stood beside me, then paced the room while I leaned one elbow on a pillow, lounging on a bed. You casually removed your bra underneath your blouse telling me something funny, distracting me with a story so I wouldn't imagine your flawless breasts under your clothes. I couldn't peek at your naked breasts but your flaunting allowed me to imagine. With your body so close to me, both of us eager, I could've grabbed you, pulled you to me, lifted your blouse above my head, filled my mouth *con tu pecho delicioso.* Reminiscing, I sigh, regretting my cowardice.

We tease more, feeding each other ice cream, sweet Mexican vanilla ice cream doused with hot, chocolate fudge. We burst with each spoonful, filling up on sugar. We eat *pan dulce,* fresh, fluffy bread, elated for hours from sugar's euphoria.

The way I love you remains an act of language. Words, narrative, myth — all my dreams convey the way I would have loved you.

I lick your lips, your labia, smother your vulva with a drenched tongue. I swallow your mouth into mine, juices stirring nuclei into one. I devour you, your liquid for my body which longs to possess you through your sweet fluid. Outside the sun and moon meet briefly, compressing desire for one hundred more years. Faithfully. In your room I will meet you with an awkward hand, unsure of your hunger. A hundred years pass in each second — I have craved you since the summer night the planets embraced outside your window.

In myths, I invent you. I consume you, shroud you, pierce you with fingers, fist, arms, head, legs, a whole body seeking you, immigrating to your womb, safe inside you, in darkness where you shine a golden beam outside of me who is buried in you. The one you longed for lies immersed, unharmed in you. You will bear me daily, your spoken words are my words like spears ascending from inside you where I live because I have nowhere else to be. There is nowhere else. I buried myself there where you recreate me with your tongue, with your words.

A clumsy hand reaches for you, fragmented, in pieces, confused over what you want. I can't read you. I misread your signals. Unsure. What do you want? You never say.

You won't admit I'm a part of you. You can't admit how much we resemble each other. Tonality, timbre of voices, behavior, ideas all similar. You continue to deny how well matched we could be.

With phrases I create you. I create you here in

text. You don't exist. I never wanted you to exist. I only wanted to invent you like this, in fragments through text where the memory of you inhabits those who read this. You have no name. To name you would limit you, fetter you from all you embody. I give you your identities. I switch them when its convenient. I make you who I want you to be. And in all my invention, no matter how much I try, you don't have the skill to love, to love me as I am.

Purposefully, you draw me close, then offer nothing. I realize you never loved me.

There's nothing left to do except what I'm about to do. What you inspire me to do. It's not just the *costurera's* son or his horrors or my nightmares, or our childhood in El Pueblo, or you, or every woman who will come after you that I must expel from inside me. It's the sleepless nights, the restless dreams, the future that can't be, the one I want to brave with someone like you or maybe not you at all. We're lost, you see. Not just you and me, but all of us. We live a violent, psychic horror daily. Some of us are more fortunate. We master ways to disembody from that which is too real to face. Some keep busy, volunteering, marching, fighting for principles. Some work sixteen-hour days with no time to think, to be. Some write away the pain. Or try to.

We're cowards, you and I. We're cowards stuck, immobile.

I want you to read me. In bed. The way you did when you contrived your love for me. You read erotic poetry, *en español*, about a woman's eyes as green as a forest's heart. I want to hear faith in your voice, in your stories, how you resurrect hope. As you read, your hand massages my neck, pushing my head to your shoulder. I'm at peace. You finish a poem and turn over to lie on your stomach. I grab a peeled orange and squeeze its juice across your back. You quiver from its coolness. You smile.

You're standing on a pier. Your figure tiny in the distance, but I recognize you in your white, wool coat. You're alone. You look over the wooden scaffold where you lean your body, elbows bent, fists pressed against chin to hold up your head. You're lost in some memory. You behold foaming waves, their white froth spewing. I watch you for a long time. You don't move. Finally, you drop your hands to your sides, putting them in your pockets. You look around wondering if anyone is watching you. You can't see me because I drop behind a column in front of a store. You spot a lonely seagull, lolling on the pier. You start to follow the seagull, it reaches the end of the pier then flies away. Now you throw your head up, eyes charting the bird. Suddenly, you fling your arms up, hold them apart and above your body at an angle towards the sky as if to offer yourself to the heavens. Your fingers are spread open catching the sun's rays. The gesture means you want to fly, but you can't. You're anchored to the earth. So you stand with arms up and open, embracing the sky. Yours is not a lonely gesture. You move gracefully. I envy you. I envy how you found reasons to live again. All your gestures show me how you found religion transparent in waves, seagulls, the sky.

This is why I love her, continue to love her secretly. I alternate between fleeting joy and disdain. When I watch her, I'm pleased she's so alive, but I regret she doesn't laugh for me. I have a photograph of her, sprawled on a pier. It's late summer. She wears shorts and a white cotton sweatshirt with holes in the sleeves. Her legs are tanned golden and luxurious. She smiles into the camera. She smiles for a lover. I'm not sure why she gave me a photo which caught her elation for another lover. I scrutinize the photo sometimes and think about how long I have known her, she who smiles for other lovers.

Desire as anomaly. A detour into longing. A

mutation from the past encoded in the future. There is no break with the past. It lies in front of you always, waiting to happen one more time, waiting for you to repeat yourself with someone you're sure you've met before.

I don't know if I was insane. Temporarily insane, or just insane. My act seemed like a source of sanity. I can't tell you when it happened. The murder. You'll have to trace the clues I leave behind in this text. I can't reveal too much. Not because I won't, but because I'm not sure I remember. I can tell you how I did it, how I took pleasure in the act, clubbing him to death, a limp body unto death.

When it happened doesn't matter. You may not believe me, the hysteric who invokes myth, reinvents truth. My hysteria tells you this part of the story. I sometimes lack the ability to discern what is real, or unreal, what I imagine to be true, or what I've made up to entertain myself, to pass away dreary hours and days. What is invisible is as alive and true to me as the visible.

I ask myself if this happened? I repress the memory, or suspect I do.

It was a day, like during childhood, when I would awaken on my twin bed next to an open window with a netted screen. I am engulfed in a nightmare so real I can't wake myself. A rainstorm cools a humid night. There's no breeze, only stillness. Torrential rainfall feeds and nourishes green pine trees and Bermuda grass. It's not summer, it's winter. In winter, balmy air stifles your breath and wool sweaters break your skin in a heat rash. Suddenly, by morning, a cold freeze will find you stranded with the same thin wool sweater. The unpredictability of the weather, they say, is what drives some people crazy.

Before me, water falls on his bloody body, washing sins down a gutter. My short brown hair drips wet around my face cleansing me and purifying him in death. I beat over and over, first his head, cracking sounds resonate as I smash his skull. His face becomes shapeless and mushy like jelly. Back, abdomen, and ribs cave in to muffled whacks beneath a cotton sweatshirt. A pool of blood spews from his head, a red-soaked runny ball spills from his matted hair. He lies in the alley, motionless, mutilated.

Twice in the night, I wake. My body is soaked, the sheets damp, my skin cold from air through the open window. More vivid nightmares. Asleep again, a soft scream wakes me. I'm on the floor. My right cheek twitches. I've fallen far from the bed, on the other side of the room, next to the door. Pushing up with my arms, I stand, stumble dizzy to the bathroom, smash a right foot against the corner of the door. In bed, my foot stings. For weeks, I will hobble.

My desire for you is endless, but I will it, this desire, fostered in what you give and what you hold back. I want to lie down beside you. I want pleading to end, but I won't end it, I want hallucinations to disappear, but they won't. Do you realize what it's like to yearn for you, every second of every day, to hear your voice in my head when I wake in the morning? When I sleep, I don't dream of you, there are no dreams of you to comfort me at night. Only nightmares, blood-drenched, nightmares. An axe swings, lands on my back, splits me open, my spine breaks. My skull fractured, brains spill on concrete, blood flows, I'm emptied out. Depleted. Now I'll have serenity. My mind won't be muddled or ensnared with you. I'm emptied of a brain to be clear again. But recurring visions bring no shelter. There is no peace when I sleep.

Sometimes, you appear, you stand back, distant, as if studying a movie screen but affected by the motion, the story on the screen invites you. You go home when its over, despair will not have blemished you, except superficially. The lover's misery on the screen only skims your senses, like a stranger's touch in a crowded bus. You, the impartial observer, washing your arm, cleansing the body with water to erase the skin's memory of an encounter. That's how you act. The one who is uninvolved, the one who restricts her passion to the certainty of a romance novel. You won't love, can't risk love. You fear loving someone like me, a woman whose sorrow follows her everywhere.

But you invite me back. You invite me only to convince me how wrong we are for each other. I'm corrupted again, taken in by your ambivalence, taken in by you.

I believed you had changed, or had wanted to. I believed you weren't afraid to give. But you withhold. You give nothing. You treat me like an idiot. You even said it once. *"No seas tonta, tonta,"* you joked. Pleased with your playfulness, I chuckled.

A friend informs me you're not answering your phone. You're never home. I haven't called. I don't call. I write letters, cards, poems. I send some, keep others. The letters I send, you don't answer. No word from you. Nothing. You give nothing. I'm addicted to the abuse of silence, to love withheld. My self-betrayal is embedded in the lover who refuses me. I foolishly anticipate your love. I wait. Past midnight, I wait. Months pass before I phone you, so sure yearning will end. I make myself sick. I'm sick, possessed by you. I hallucinate. I see people I recognize but their

faces have changed. Ominous faces, distrust-
ful faces. I vomit from some illness without a
name. A feverish body shakes. Under the covers, in my bed, I gape at a ceiling. Empty.
Cold. White. I close my eyes to hunt for your
face. Two months have passed since I left, but
you appear before me vividly. Visions of you
will free me from insanity.

My mother told me about her cousin's son, a
boy who trusted his powers, saint-like, god-
given. *"Era como el niño Fidencio, el curan-
dero,"* my mother said, his body frail, his face
angelic, but worried. A permanent frown on
his forehead thwarted inner peace. Convinced
he let his mother die from a disease which ate
her marrow, his miracles ended. The angelic
boy thought he failed her, the woman who
bore him with the breath he wanted to give
back. After she abandoned her life-form, he
lost faith. He couldn't understand she wasn't
dead, that she lives somewhere else now, in
peace. *"Ya no pudo curar, ni adivinar,"* my
mother told me.

I wear a frown like his on my forehead. Permanently. I put it there when I was too young
to become the frown that would frighten people away. Like you. You see a vehement face,
not worry. My madness frightens you. Sometimes I imagine your happiness could be my
miracle. But like my mother's cousin's son, I
too lost faith in saint-like powers. You fear me,

parts of me, my violent fury. But I fear you too. I fear your gentleness, your warmth, I fear your seasoned, fiery kiss. I am as afraid of pleasure that could last.

I invent you daily, hungering, awakened from sleep to hold you lying on me. My hands smooth down your spine, its flesh tingles. I draw circles on your back with teasing fingers. Your lips curve into your off center smile. You arch your back, full breasts fall above me, bursting. Opulent, straight hair covers your shoulders, frames your face.

Do you remember when you drove me to your father's village? It was as if you wanted to take a shortcut to your past, to my discovery of you. What could have taken years to explain, you showed me instead in one brief week-end in a place where houses were big, old, and yellow-brown like the adobe used to build them. Lying in a motel bed you whispered stories that drew me so close I didn't notice you might have been nervous about what we planned to do. I wanted to stop you, to ask why you wandered around the room, until finally, you had courage to throw your body against mine, flaunting its supreme beauty. I blame myself for beginning to love you in a way that can only be expressed on paper.

You exhaust me, consume me; I sink deeper. You have scribbled on a post-card, "I'm happy." The report meant to drive a wedge between us. I try to forget you and all you represent. If you turned to look at me, if you only glanced toward me, that would be enough to send me spinning, that would be enough for days of fantasy.

The days don't let me rest. I wear myself out. More hellish images, more nightmares. More blood-stained hands. It's as if I prowl at night committing acts I don't remember. Mornings, I awake, my mind refreshed, my flesh bruised. I can't blame the woman from El Pueblo anymore, I can't blame *la costurera's* son. I can't even blame myself. But I keep trying to lay blame somewhere hoping that will release me.

My dreams trick me. You overtook me last night in what could have been another bad dream, but instead you kissed me lavishly and in the dream's brevity, I was fulfilled. Today I'm fulfilled with the way you wrapped your legs around me. You almost never come to me anymore, so you can see why I was surprised to have you with me, not letting go, clutching me, clinging to my naked legs. You removed my clothes, kissing my torso, licking my skin, biting my nipples. You buried your face between my thighs and your hot tongue made me cry from wanting you so long. When I awoke to glimpse another's back, not yours, beside me, I was content she was with me and that the loving I'd had with you had not sent her away. But soon, she too would leave.

Forgiveness doesn't come to me naturally, but it could save me from more blood-stained hands. I can't blame you or women like you anymore. You refuse me, shun me, reject me. You think I'm crazy. I am. Crazy to think someone else will do for me what I must do for myself.

I'm tortured daily. I create torture. I'm stuck with no other way, no doorways out, I live in self-effacing pity. I will release you. I can't look for you. I can't blame you because you won't choose me. How can you choose someone who won't offer anything but a few weekends of lust and then not even friendship.

You were a symptom, a symptom of my irrevocable illness. I warned you how I fell in love with women easily. I was careful to warn you about my dishonesty, my carelessness. There is no cure for my illness, the insanity I rehearse. Nothing will change me, not even you, my beautiful symptom, the one who will not judge me harshly.

To watch a lover go, over and over, different lovers go and you can't hold them, you never learned how to ask someone to stay; instead, you lead her to the door, drive her out, satisfied she's gone. To feel self-satisfied because what you suspected came true, to feel so sure of your unhappiness, to affirm your own discontent so much that you know you don't deserve peace. You don't deserve love. Never did. Only harm. Repeatedly, you do this, invite into your life those who humiliate you. You welcome it. Beseech it. Expect it and nothing else. Not gentleness. Not love. I am accustomed to pain. Pain is my source of pleasure. The woman from El Pueblo, I craved her insults, begged for punishment to feel something puncture deadened flesh.

There are no cures. People like us can't be cured. Remedies don't exist, they haven't been invented. Only behaviors can be changed through habitual prayer. One learns to pray to someone or something, anything so long as a response is imagined in one's head, but there are no treatments for those of us who track the pleasure of pain, whether inflicting or receiving, instead repression is learned; one prays for passion to fade, for dreaded obsessions to dissipate, that's the only comfort. Or act again. Fall victim to selfishness. Again. Ache again so much that death would be easier, softer. You will welcome death, its peace.

Epilogue

When the trial ended, the loud rapist was sentenced to thirty years. No one accepted it. His lawyer, Pelón, appealed, wanting to expose more from Ermila's past, he said. The Associate Justice wrote that Chencho could cross-examine Ermila. The loud rapist wanted to prove she had men everywhere, in cars, in houses, in fields. He said she picked men up in grocery stores, in parking lots, in bars, on the street. Everybody saw how she took men everywhere and now she complained as if she were a virgin, he thought. Chencho declared he'd win, arguing, she was the liar. The other four in the group came away unpunished, ready to avenge the loud rapist's sentence. The four paraded out of the courtroom heroically celebrating their release and the loud rapist's upcoming appeal.

He was in Los Angeles when I spotted him. There are no coincidences, after all. I sighted the loud rapist alone in a bar, drinking a mug of beer. I recognized him immediately, his body thinner, frailer, after a short year in prison. I studied him closely from across the room. He didn't greet me. He never had, even when I attended the trial, he never saw me.

For weeks, I observed him. When the bar closed evenings, he scouted and prowled in the parking lot, waiting until he made eye contact with some older man. One morning, on the local news, white-robed men carried on a stretcher his blood drenched body covered with a thin white sheet. The loud rapist had been beaten to death. The bartender, who stepped outside to throw away trash from the last evening, found him lying face up in the muddy alley behind the bar. A shapeless face with shocked eyes had a gaping mouth stuffed with something. The police promised to investigate, but they wouldn't. The murderer, unless he struck again, wouldn't be found. They filed the case away without much concern. None of them cared about a murder in the back alley of a "pervert bar", they said, and none of them wanted to track the murderer's traces, imprints which shocked those who saw the carved figure. Flattened, pale testicles with dried cakes of blood were jammed into Inocencio's mouth. Reporters and ambulance drivers would have nightmares, for years, tossing nervously, conjuring up an image of a boy's limp body.

And Ermila, Ermila disappeared. No one knew if she left town or if she vanished with the tide on the Gulf coast. One evening, when a red-orange sun suspended itself on the water, Ermila drifted alone on the beach. And then, she wasn't seen again. This happened almost a year after the trial ended. The events would become foggy memories. Ermila couldn't stay in a place that deliberately forgot her outrage. She vowed to go, but she didn't know where, or when, or how.

Did Ermila dive into the sea that night? Or did she fill a vinyl yellow suitcase with clothes to catch a bus going south to find her grandmother's village? No one knows. Maybe the men who didn't go to prison, the ones determined to punish her, maybe they found her. Maybe they taught her never to open her mouth against men again. I want to believe she's living in Mexico, safe with women who can care for her. I want to believe Ermila has forgotten the trial, its terror. Her life has purpose. Someone caresses her, someone she loves, someone who accepts her in a better time, a better place.

I saw her name printed in a newspaper like the first time I'd read it after the rape. Ermila. The bones of a woman dug up in a cove on the beach. People in town identified the bones as hers. Everyone had wanted her silent. They wished her silence in decaying bones. For me, Ermila lives happily in her grandmother's village in Mexico. Children surround her as she weaves stories about el norte and how it makes some men evil, others greedy.

I'm cursed with a memory for detail. I'm sure stark details keep me awake at night forcing me to plot shadows on ceilings and walls. To forget, that's my goal, my challenge, my promise to myself. Memories arrive slowly like a gray photograph taking shape in a dark room, then I must stop the print from over-exposure by shoving the image into something less organic, like chemicals. Every mark becomes magnified and fixed in darkness. The photograph, with its own spirit, reminds you how each detail buried inside you has a life private and sequestered.

I choose this past — my mother's strong arms as she bent to pick cotton, my father's fried chicken when we came home from *la pisca*. I remember my sisters dressing and painting their faces, my brother strolling beside me. I remember my *güelita's empanadas*.

❏

Long before I decided to leave again, I left. One day, I kept driving until I drove so long and far, I hadn't noticed the horizon's changing colors. At dusk, I rode into swirling orange-navy sunsets, at dawn, marbled ivory skies awakened the hunter in me searching for a home, migrating through deserts and mountains, leaving gulf waters and dreams that tormented. It became clear to me that the cruelty I'd lived with her finally caused me to feel kindness, to feel pity, to realize love takes many forms.

Desire for her exhausted me, exhausts me still as I lie awake at night, wondering, asking myself why I couldn't stay, or why she couldn't come with me. And I suppose we both know our answers, have memorized deceitful explanations to repeat silently, convincingly. Our hearts, so damaged, were incapable of offering the kind of love that sustains lovers through years, through lifetimes.

This part of the story has to be over, even though I don't believe in endings. I believe in the imagination, its pleasure indelible, transgressive, a dream.